"We'd better get moving," Sam said. "We have a lot to do."

"I'm with you," Joe said, frowning up at the lights. "I just hope the power doesn't go out before we're finished."

With Wishbone in the lead, Sam, Joe, and David made their way toward the auditorium. Their footsteps echoed in the empty hall. Sam started to get that creepy feeling again. *This is silly!* Sam thought. *I'm getting jumpy at the sound of my own feet!*

Opening the auditorium doors, Joe directed Sam and David through. Then he and Wishbone followed them.

The lights flickered, then dimmed. A second later, as the doors clanked shut behind them, the lights went out. Sam froze. She peered into the blackness of the windowless auditorium. Her heartbeat pounded loudly in her ears. Reaching out with one hand, she searched for a row of seats, or a wall. But her hand only sliced through the black air.

Her breathing turned heavy, almost drowning out the sound of her heartbeat. Goose bumps shot up her arms. Sam didn't know how she knew, but she knew. Something wasn't right.

"Joe! David!" Sam whispered. "I think someone else is in here with us!"

Books in the
WISHBONE™ Mysteries series:

Books in the **WISHBONE**
SUPER Mysteries series:

*coming soon

STAGE INVADER

by Vivian Sathre

WISHBONE™ created by Rick Duffield

Big Red Chair Books™, *A Division of* **Lyrick Publishing**™

This book is a work of fiction. The characters, incidents, and dialogues are products of the author's imagination and are not to be construed as real. Any resemblance to actual events or persons, living or dead, is entirely coincidental.

 Big Red Chair Books™, *A Division of Lyrick Publishing*™
300 E. Bethany Drive, Allen, Texas 75002

©1999 Big Feats! Entertainment

Edited by Pam Pollack

Copy edited by Jonathon Brodman

Cover concept and design by Lyle Miller

Interior illustrations by Kathryn Yingling

Wishbone photograph by Carol Kaelson

Library of Congress Catalog Card Number: 98-87206

ISBN: 1-57064-563-9

First printing: February 1999

10 9 8 7 6 5 4 3 2 1

Printed in the United States of America

For my theater pals—
Marilee and Walt, Jana and Sam, and Roger

CAST OF CHARACTERS

David Barnes: Joe Talbot and Wishbone's neighbor and close friend. David is the special-effects and sound technician for the Sequoyah Middle School eighth-grade production of *Grease.*

Nathan Barnes: David Barnes's dad, and all-around nice guy.

McKenzie Crane: The girlfriend of Ryan Matthews, the male lead in *Grease.*

Wanda Gilmore: Next-door neighbor to Ellen Talbot, Joe Talbot, and the handsome Jack Russell terrier. Wanda loves flowers, but she dislikes having *the dog* digging near them.

Amanda Hollings: Classmate of Joe Talbot, Samantha Kepler, and David Barnes. Amanda is the choreographer for *Grease* (she plans the dance routines).

Damont Jones: Classmate of Joe, Sam, and David's. Damont is sometimes called "Damontser" by Wishbone.

Samantha Kepler: Stage manager for *Grease.* "Sam" is best friend to Joe and David—and she is one of Wishbone's favorite people. She is particularly good at scratching the Jack Russell's ears. Her dad owns a pizza parlor.

Walter Kepler: Sam's dad, and the owner of Pepper Pete's Pizza Parlor.

Rachel Lee: Eighth-grader at Sequoyah. Rachel is in charge of costumes, and she plays Rizzo, one of the teenaged high-school students in *Grease*.

Ryan Matthews: One of the two top dogs in *Grease*. Ryan plays the lead male role of Danny.

Robin Santia: Classmate of Joe, Sam, and David's. In *Grease*, Robin plays Frenchie. Frenchie hangs around with Danny and his crowd. She becomes friends with Sandy, the new girl in school.

Crystal Simms: The other top dog in *Grease*. Crystal plays the lead female role of Sandy, the new girl in school.

Ellen Talbot: Top dog at the Talbot house. Ellen is the keeper of Wishbone's snacks.

Joe Talbot: Wishbone's best friend. Joe is the lighting technician and set designer (he plans the stage backdrops and creates the props) for *Grease*.

Justin Wallingford: Eighth-grader at Sequoyah. Justin is the director of *Grease*.

Wishbone: *The noble dog*. Wishbone plays Frenchie's Guardian Angel in *Grease*.

FROM THE BIG RED CHAIR . . .

Oh . . . hi! Wishbone here. You caught me right in the middle of some of my favorite things—books. Let me welcome you to the WISHBONE MYSTERIES. In each story, I help my human friends solve a puzzling mystery. In *STAGE INVADER*, my pals and I have important roles in a school play. Sam, as stage manager, runs into problems and looks to Super Dog, yours truly, for help.

The story takes place in the winter, during the same time period as the events that you'll see in the second season of my WISHBONE television show. In this story, Joe is fourteen, and he and his friends are in the eighth grade. Like me, they are always ready for adventure . . . and a good mystery.

You're in for a real treat, so pull up a chair and a snack and sink your teeth into *STAGE INVADER*!

Chapter One

Wishbone raced in a circle around one of the pink flamingos in the yard of his neighbor, Wanda Gilmore. It was a warmer than usual winter day. Wishbone stopped at a flower bed to get in a few power digs. "The smell . . . oh, the smell . . . I just love the smell!" he said, with each toss of dirt from his paws.

It would have been better if there were flowers to dig up, but Wishbone knew that would have to wait until spring, when Wanda filled her flower beds.

Wishbone shook himself from head to tail to remove any dirt on his white-with-brown-and-black-spots coat. He looked from one flamingo to another and wagged his tail. "Now, remember, if Wanda asks, you didn't see me. Got it?"

As usual, the flamingos didn't move or speak.

"Great! I knew I could count on you guys."

Wishbone trotted back toward the house next door, where he lived with his best friend, Joe Talbot, and Joe's mom, Ellen. The dog's inner clock told him it was nearly time for Joe's classes to end at school. That meant it was almost time for rehearsal to start. The eighth-graders at Sequoyah Middle School were practicing to put on a really cool play, *Grease*. It was a musical about a bunch of friends in high school in 1959. They were cool kids who wore grease in their hair and weren't afraid to be who they really were. When a new girl, Sandy, came to the school, she learned to be true to herself, too—after she caught the eye of the coolest of the guys, a boy named Danny. The girls were super cool—so cool that one of them, Frenchie, had a Guardian Angel. That angel would be played by none other than the handsome Jack Russell terrier, Wishbone! That meant he got to be at all the rehearsals. At school! With no one shooing him away.

I am one lucky dog! Wishbone thought. *It's not every day that a dog gets a free pass to get inside school. If I could only find a way to make the pass permanent!* He pointed his nose at the sidewalk, his tail at the sky, and aimed himself in the direction of the school.

Wishbone had an important part onstage, while his close friends were working hard behind the scenes. Joe was in charge of the set design—creating and building all scene backgrounds and props—and stage lighting. That meant he had to be at all the rehearsals. Joe's two best human friends were at the rehearsals too. David Barnes was in charge of special effects and sound for the play. He was a whiz at that stuff. Samantha Kepler—"Sam" to her friends—had a really tough job. She was the stage manager. It was up to Sam to make sure everything was organized during rehearsals and running smoothly by opening night. Sam had a big job, but she still found time to give Wishbone terrific ear scratches!

As the middle school came into view, Wishbone heard a woman's voice in the distance.

"Jinx! Ji-inx!"

"Jinx?" Wishbone slowed.

"Ji-iinx!" the voice called again.

"With a name like that, it *has* to be a cat." Wishbone glanced from side to side as he trotted on. He lowered his voice. "Calling all canines. Feline alert. Suspect is armed and dangerous. Outfitted with small, furry paws that hide very sharp weapons. Approach cautiously."

Wishbone quickly sniffed his way across the lawn of the post office. Then, glancing both ways and not seeing any cars, Wishbone cautiously stepped into the street.

"Hey—watch out!" a man yelled.

A pair of bicycle tires zoomed past Wishbone's head. He jumped back to the curb. Pebbles from the street sprayed him.

"Hey, pal!" Wishbone barked, as the helmeted rider pedaled out of sight. "This is a school zone. Slow down!"

Wishbone was sure he'd checked both ways before stepping into the street. *Hey! Maybe I've been jinxed by Jinx! I hope that streaking bike isn't the beginning of a streak of bad luck.*

After looking both ways again, Wishbone stepped off the curb. When he was halfway across the street, a huge white cat jumped in front of him. Opening its mouth wide, it hissed in Wishbone's face.

Wishbone stared into the big pink mouth, full of sharp white teeth. Slowly, he lowered his head. He noticed the cat's puffed-out tail. "I should warn you," Wishbone barked. "I've been specially trained to deal with felines."

The cat hissed again, then swiped at Wishbone's nose.

Wishbone jumped back. "Let me guess—Jinx, right?" Bravely, Wishbone took a small step forward.

The cat raced for the nearest tree.

"Just another exciting moment in the world of Wishbone." With his tail held high, the Jack Russell terrier trotted toward the main entrance of Sequoyah Middle School. He lowered his voice. "Calling all canines. Suspect has positioned himself in big oak near the post office."

Before Wishbone reached the front lawn of Sequoyah Middle School, the double doors burst open and kids rushed out.

Wishbone broke into a run. "The Guardian Angel is coming through!" He tried weaving his way in and out of the oncoming crowd. The sea of legs and sneakers held him back. "This is like trying to dogpaddle upstream. Excuse me, people—I need to get in! Hey!" He quickly danced away from a huge sneaker about to step on him. "Watch the dog, fella."

This is not working, Wishbone thought.

Turning around, the dog started to walk *with* the flow of foot traffic. "If you can't beat 'em, join 'em."

He worked his way to one side of the crowd. Then he separated himself from the large group and ran behind the school building to the door that led directly backstage.

"Great bushes back here," he said, glancing around. "I should hang out here more often."

"Helllooo!" Wishbone barked at the door. "The *dog* needs to get in."

Samantha Kepler stared into her locker, but her mind wasn't on which books she needed for homework. Sam was worried about the school play. This was the first year there was going to be a completely student-run production. She was in charge of everything and everyone. She had to know where the props, costumes, and even the actors were at all times. Sam was eager to prove the students could handle the responsibility. Today was Monday; the play opened Friday. She wished she could be sure everything and everyone would be ready.

After grabbing her jacket and history book, Sam walked down the hall to the auditorium. She tugged open one of the heavy double doors and stepped inside. The stage was framed on both sides by a thick red curtain, and at the back of the stage was a wall with a black backdrop curtain in front of it. There was also a

staircase on either side of the stage, going from the house floor—where the audience sat—up to the stage.

Sam walked down the aisle to the front-row seats. There, Justin Wallingford, the director, was studying a script. His curly blond hair, in need of a trim, hung over his eyes. A pencil rested behind his right ear. One side of the collar on his blue shirt was sticking up. No one would ever guess by looking at his rumpled appearance that he wanted everything in the play to be perfect. "Hi," Sam said.

Justin looked up from his script. "Hi. I know I said we were going to rehearse the big dance scene today. But I think I'd like to start off with the scene where Danny and Sandy meet at school for the first time." Danny and Sandy were the two lead characters in the cast, played by Ryan Matthews and Crystal Simms.

"Okay." Sam was used to Justin's last-minute changes. She started toward the stairs at the left side of the stage.

"Oh, wait," Justin said. "Before we start, could you tell Crystal I need to talk to her?"

"Sure." Sam looked up at the stage. Most of the cast seemed to be there—except Crystal.

That's odd, Sam thought. *Crystal is never late. She's always the first one to arrive at rehearsal. She always gets her lines right—I've never even had to prompt her.* Then Sam saw Ryan, the boy who played Danny.

Ryan was sitting near the back wall of the stage, on the low, five-step bleachers that were used in the dance number. He and his girlfriend, McKenzie Crane, were snacking on cookies and laughing to each other. Sam wished that they were going over Danny's lines instead. Sam had fed him his lines so often that *she* almost had his part memorized. "Have either of you seen Crystal?"

"No. Not since lunch." Ryan smiled.

Sam looked at McKenzie, who shook her head without answering. The girl looked just like Ryan. She had shiny, straight black hair and big brown eyes.

"Thanks." Sam was almost at the far left side of the stage when, in the wings, she saw Joe there.

She passed Wishbone on the way. He was trotting toward Ryan.

"Wishbone, are you after those cookies?" Sam teased.

The Jack Russell terrier looked at Sam and wagged his tail, but he didn't stop.

Sam found her other best friend, David Barnes, the sound technician, next to Joe. David was kneeling down, testing a tape in his cassette player. Joe was leaning against a tall stack of chairs. Both boys had their backs to her. "Hi, guys."

As Joe turned around, his straight brown hair brushed across his forehead. "Hi, Sam."

David turned and echoed Joe's greeting. A smile crinkled his face.

"Have either of you seen Crystal?" Sam asked. As she spoke, she walked to the left end of the backstage wall. A curtained doorway, used only by cast and crew, opened up to two hallways beyond. Sam pulled the curtain back and looked straight down the first hallway, but she saw no sign of Crystal. This first hallway had a door on the left leading directly outside of the building. Farther down the hall there was a door to the right going into the dressing room. Then, Sam glanced to the right, down the second hallway—again, no sign of Crystal. This second hallway ran for the entire length of the back wall of the stage. It  had one door on the left, leading to the storage room. Next to the storage-room door were two folding doors that opened up to a wardrobe closet. Those doors were usually open.

Joe and David shook their heads.

"Didn't you tell her that rehearsal was going to start earlier today?" Joe asked.

Sam nodded. "I called everyone yesterday morning." She checked her watch and frowned. "Rehearsal starts in a few minutes." She looked down at David's cassette player. "Oh, David! Is your sign here?" Sam was referring to the sign David was making for the play. Every time the curtain opened, the sign would drop down from the ceiling of the stage. It would remind the audience that it was the 1950s. David's sign was in the shape of Greased Lightning, the hot rod that belonged to one of the teenagers in *Grease*.

"My dad's going to help me bring the sign to school tomorrow morning," David said.

"Great!" *That's one thing I don't have to worry about. If David's handling it, it's as good as done.* "I can't wait to see it. You always come up with such awesome ideas."

"Thanks," David said, his brown eyes shining.

Sam turned to Joe. "Do you need any help with the scenery props?"

Joe ran a hand through his hair. "I'll finish them up tomorrow right after our rehearsal. Then do you want to help David and me move them into the auditorium?"

"Sure. Pick me up at Pepper Pete's. We can have pizza before we move the props." Sam smiled. Then she hurried into the hallway, stepping through a ribbon of sunshine created by the propped-open back door. Sam went into the dressing room. She put her history book and jacket on the makeup counter next to the coats and backpacks belonging to the other students. *No sign of Crystal in here, either.* Sam left the dressing room and turned down the other hallway. She stopped at the wardrobe closet that was built into the wall. The costumes still weren't on the rack.

Justin, the director, leaned through the doorway leading from the stage. "I haven't seen Crystal," he called out to Sam. "Have you got everybody else?"

As Sam headed Justin's way, Rachel Lee hurried around the corner, nearly bumping into Sam. Rachel played Rizzo, one of the featured characters, the leader of the girlfriends in *Grease*. She was also in charge of the costumes.

"Look, Sam," Rachel said. "I found a bunch of real 1950s-style ponytail scarves!"

"That's great, Rachel," Sam said. "Are the costumes ready?"

"Wednesday . . . Thursday at the latest." Rachel held up her hand, as if taking an oath. "I promise."

"Thursday is the dress rehearsal!" Sam shook her head. "I'm counting on you, Rachel," Sam reminded her.

"I know." Rachel nodded quickly. "I'd better get these things to the wardrobe closet before rehearsal starts."

As Rachel left, Sam turned and came face to face with Justin. In talking to Rachel, Sam had forgotten about him.

"Sam, I really want to get started."

"Crystal's not here. I can't find her anywhere," Sam said.

Justin glanced across the stage. "Well, let's start, anyway. Ryan can pretend Crystal's there." Justin turned to the kids onstage. "Listen up, everybody," he called. "We're starting rehearsal without Crystal."

Immediately, Amanda Hollings, the choreographer—the one who planned and created the dance routines—stepped forward. Like Sam, Amanda had long hair. But while Sam had straight blond hair, Amanda's hair was black.

"*I* can stand in for her," Amanda said. "*I* know all her lines."

That's right! Sam remembered. Amanda had tried out for the starring role of Sandy, too. She'd bragged around school that she knew all the lines by heart—before tryouts. Amanda was sure she was going to get the part. Then when tryouts came, she lost the role to Crystal.

"Okay, Amanda." Justin nodded. "Get ready for your entrance." Justin headed off the stage to take a seat in the front row.

Sam looked around for her script. Then she realized she'd left it in her locker. She hurried backstage and grabbed one from a bookshelf in the dressing room. Then she went and took a seat next to Justin.

All the actors took their places. Justin nodded, signaling for them to begin. Suddenly, everyone was in character.

Rachel, as Rizzo, walked out onto the stage and said, "Hey, Danny. I've got a surprise for you."

"Oh, yeah? What?" Ryan replied, playing Danny.

"No, no," Justin broke in, stopping the scene. "Say it like this, Rachel. . . ." He raised his voice to sound like a girl's. "'I got a surprise for *you*.'"

Sam shook her head. Justin was *such* a perfectionist. How would they ever finish their rehearsal on time?

Rachel repeated her line just the way Justin had instructed her.

"Oh, yeah? What?" Ryan repeated.

Amanda, playing Sandy, entered the stage at Danny's back. "Hello, Danny," said Amanda.

Ryan was facing Rachel and turned around to see who had called his name.

"Sandy!" Ryan's eyes widened. "What are you doing here? Why aren't you . . . uh . . . uh . . ." Ryan looked blankly down at Sam. "I'm sorry. I forgot my line!"

"'Why aren't you at the Saint Bernadette school?'" Rachel teased him good-naturedly.

"Right, right." Ryan nodded. Then he closed his eyes for a moment and took a deep breath. It was almost as if he were trying to burn the line into his eyelids. He certainly seemed to have a problem memorizing his part.

From the corner of her eye, Sam caught a glimpse of McKenzie. She was glaring at Ryan. Sam wondered if she was upset that Ryan had forgotten his lines again.

Suddenly the auditorium door burst open, and the noise interrupted Sam's thoughts. She and the others turned to look.

"Crystal!" Sam said. "Where have you been?"

WISHBONE'S STAR-QUALITY DICTIONARY

For Anyone (or Any Dog) Who Wants to Bone Up on Stage Terms

backdrop   curtain very near the back wall of the stage that lets actors walk from one side of the stage to the other without being seen by the audience

backstage   the part of the theater not seen by the audience; also called "offstage"

behind the stage the area behind the back wall of the stage. At Sequoyah Middle School, a crisscrossing hallway runs behind the stage.

cable   strong rope, or wires, twisted together. It runs from the control panel to above the stage, and is used to raise and lower things.

control panel   a group of switches and pulleys located on a side wall of the stage. It controls the stage lights, the cables above the stage, and the stage curtain.

cue   action or word that tells the actor to begin his or her part

house   audience area inside the theater

onstage   the area of the stage that is seen by the audience—my favorite place to be!

prop	short for "property"; any piece of furniture or small item used onstage for a play
pulley	a simple machine made from rope and a grooved wheel; used to raise and lower things
set	the general look of the stage area, with scenery in place
set design	scenery for the stage
stage left	Helllooo! This can be confusing! It's not the part of the stage on the audience's left. It's the part of the stage on the *actor's* left as he or she stands onstage and looks out at the audience.
stage manager	person in charge of the arrangements of the stage during the rehearsals and the performances of a play
stage right	the part of the stage on the actor's right as he or she stands onstage and faces the audience
storage room	a room near the stage area used to store extra sets, props, tools, or anything that might be needed to put on a play
storage seat	a sturdy box with a lid that can be used as a seat, or as a temporary storage area for small props that will be needed onstage during a play
wings	both sides of the stage that are out of sight of the audience—these wings don't have anything to do with flying!

Chapter Two

Sam was relieved to see the tall, blond-haired girl. Crystal stopped and looked around. She had a look of total shock on her face. "Sam!" she gasped. "You told me rehearsal started at four o'clock."

"*Three-thirty*," Sam said.

"Oh, no! You must've been wondering where I was. Sorry, everyone."

Sam was puzzled. "I told you rehearsal was at *four o'clock?*"

Crystal made her way toward the stage stairs. "Oh, don't worry about it. You had so much to do, calling everyone and all. By the time you got around to me, you probably just made a little mistake."

Did I? Sam wondered, as the cast got ready to start the scene again. She had been so busy with the play and school

that she had been forgetting little things. Like her script in her locker. Sam tried to recall her exact words when

23

she had phoned Crystal. She couldn't. *What will I forget next?* Sam wondered. It was her job to keep everything running smoothly. And she had no one to go to for help.

Crystal dropped off her backpack in the dressing room, then came out onstage. Justin called her down to where he was sitting.

Justin looked at his watch. "Let's take a *short* break, everyone. Be back in six minutes exactly, ready to have some fun—and to make some progress. We're going to do the big dance scene."

Amanda had choreographed a great 1950s dance number for the end of the play. The entire cast was involved, with stars Ryan and Crystal dancing on the bleachers. It was a cool, rocking number that made everybody want to jump up and join in.

As soon as Justin stood up, Wishbone stood up, too, and looked over at Joe. He had been sitting by the control panel, where Joe was working. The control panel was the command center for the stage lights, the stage curtain, and the cables that traveled above the stage. They were used to raise or lower props and scenery. The control panel was offstage, stage right, and not visible to the audience.

As the stage filled with kids and buzzed with conversation, Sam hurried toward the exit at the back of the auditorium. She had just enough time to go and get a quick drink at the water fountain in the main hallway. Pushing open one of the auditorium doors, she glanced over her shoulder. She saw David walking down the stage stairs and she waved.

"Can I talk to you for a minute?" Justin asked David, when he had finished talking to Crystal.

"Sure," David replied.

Then the door shut behind Sam. Turning down the hall, Sam walked to the nearest drinking fountain. As she sipped from the arc of water, Sam looked forward to watching the kids dance.

After taking one last sip from the water fountain, Sam walked back to the auditorium. When she came through the doorway, David and Justin were standing up, deep in conversation. Justin had his back to her.

"Should we get started?" Sam called to Justin as she approached.

When Justin turned to look at Sam, David quickly headed for the stairs leading up to the stage.

"I was telling David my idea for the sign," Justin said matter-of-factly.

"But David's sign is already finished," Sam said. "He's bringing it in tomorrow. I'm sure it'll be great."

"But I know a way to make his sign even better," Justin said. "With the help of some kind of flammable composition—"

"Flammable *what?*" Sam asked.

"Fireworks," Justin explained.

"Fireworks *in school*? No way, Justin."

"How about lasers, then?"

"You can't be serious!" Sam said. "This is a middle-school play, not some big Hollywood production."

But Justin did look serious. "I can *make* it a big production," he said, continuing to look at her calmly. "I *know* I can." Then he turned and sat down.

Sam shook her head. *Justin always has such big*

ideas. And he's usually trying one way or another to get others to see things his way. Sam waved her hand in the air. "Okay," she said over the kids' voices, "break's over." She sat down next to Justin.

"Ryan, you should be at stage left," Justin said. "Crystal, you should be in the wings, stage right, ready to go on."

As the stage cleared and became silent, Crystal and Ryan took their places.

Justin nodded, signaling for Ryan to start.

Sam glanced toward the wings on the left side of the stage. Wishbone was in his spot offstage.

When Ryan spun around, Crystal entered. They started to make their way across the floor toward each other. When they met in the middle of the stage, they joined right hands. Joe shone the overhead spotlight down on them. David started the music. Looking into each other's eyes, Ryan and Crystal were supposed to move up onto the first step of the bleachers.

Ryan jumped up, but Crystal stood on the stage floor. Their hands separated, and Crystal's hands dropped to her side.

The stage went silent. For the second time that afternoon, everybody stopped and stared at Crystal.

Sam and Justin exchanged worried glances. Then Sam asked, "What's wrong?"

Crystal pointed at the bleachers. "I'm worried," she told Sam and Justin. "I know it looks great when we dance on the bleachers. But someone might get hurt on them. You know, slip and fall—twist an ankle or something."

Amanda ran out of the wings with her hands on

her hips. Before Sam and Justin could say anything, she pointed a finger at Crystal. "You've been rehearsing on them. How come you *just now* decided it might be dangerous?"

"What do you think, Sam?" Crystal asked. "Are the bleachers okay?"

Everyone looked at Sam. Sam hesitated. The bleachers looked safe. But she didn't want anyone to get hurt. *This is one of the times it would be nice to have an adult around,* Sam thought. *Someone to help me make the right decision.*

Before Sam could answer, Amanda broke in. "Oh, come on!" she said in a superior tone of voice. She clicked her tongue impatiently and stepped up to the bleachers. "You're not doing backflips or anything—you're just stepping up and down. Watch." Amanda stepped up and down the bleachers, clapping her hands and going through the routine. Sam enjoyed watching Amanda do the dance. Sam could also tell that Amanda loved being the center of attention.

"Thanks, Amanda," Crystal said sweetly. "You make it all look so easy. I'm sure I'll be able to handle it now."

Amanda stopped, her smile fading as she jumped from the bottom step. "No problem," she said, walking offstage.

Wishbone walked back and forth in front of the control panel. "Joe! Buddy! What do I have to do around here to get my after-school snack?" He looked

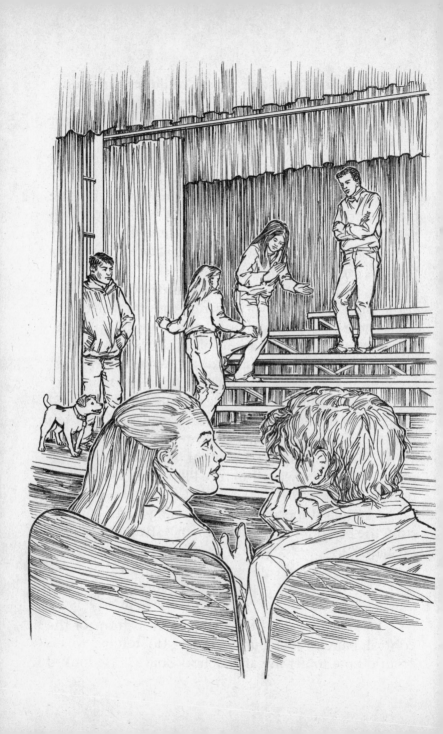

over his shoulder. "Hurry, Joe. Before they start rehearsing again." He put his front paws on Joe's leg. "Feed the dog!"

"Now I get it!" Joe said. "I forgot to give you your ginger snaps."

"Okay, everyone," Justin called from the edge of the stage. "Take your places. We're going to run through that last scene again."

"Wishbone, it's time to start," Joe said. He headed out the curtained doorway to the hall where Wishbone's bowl was kept, near the wardrobe closet. "I'll put them out, but you'll have to wait until we're done with this scene to eat. Sorry, boy."

"No problem. Hey—how about an extra ginger snap for my being so understanding?" Wishbone made his way back to the wings and sat down. The stage got silent as Ryan took his place.

"You forgot your sunglasses, Ryan," Wishbone said.

"Wait!" Crystal said from offstage. "You forgot your sunglasses."

"Helllooo!" Wishbone looked at Crystal, standing near him. "Is there an echo in here?"

As Ryan slipped the cool-looking shades over his eyes, Wishbone scratched his side.

"Those make you look hip on the outside, Ryan," the dog said. "But my nose tells me you're really, really, really nervous on the inside." Wishbone wagged his tail. "Maybe you should try doing a couple laps around the flagpole. That always seems to help me calm down."

When Justin nodded at Ryan to start, Ryan-as-Danny spun around, facing Crystal.

"Nice spin, Ryan!" Wishbone took a step closer to the edge of the wings. "But if you want to be really, really cool, well, I have this flip thing that I do. Watch." Wishbone flipped in the air. He wagged his tail. "Got your attention, huh?"

Ryan and Crystal were at opposite ends of the stage and started across the stage floor toward each other.

"Okay, maybe I can show you my routine some other time, then," Wishbone said.

Wishbone heard his stomach growl. He hadn't eaten since breakfast—if those few bites of Ryan's cookies didn't count. And a dog needed to keep up his strength on the stage. What a day this had been! Sam sure had a lot of things to keep track of—actors, props, costumes, scenery. And Justin wanted to make some Bruno-the-Doberman-sized—no, make that Saint-Bernard-sized—last-minute changes in the production.

Wishbone wagged his tail. It was lucky for the kids that Wishbone took his role of the Guardian Angel seriously. Sam was so busy that she didn't know her nose from her tail—she definitely needed a Guardian Angel. With things going the way they were, the production could use an experienced four-legged caretaker.

The overhead spotlight and music came on. Ryan and Crystal started to dance up and down the seats of the bleachers. Their feet were moving fast together.

"Hey, Ryan," Wishbone said. "Your timing is a hair off. I could give you two some pointers on coordinating four feet at once."

Wishbone looked across to the wings on the other side of the stage. He expected to see Amanda in her usual spot, practicing backstage, along with some of the other actors. But she wasn't there.

The music played faster. Wishbone knew that meant the scene was almost over. Crystal and Ryan were at the front of the stage now. Ryan raised his arm, and Crystal twirled under it as they began their exit from the stage in opposite directions, just as Amanda had shown them. The music came to an end, everyone stopped like statues, and the lights went out.

Wishbone wagged his tail. "Bravo! Bravo! Okay, snack time!" But before he could take a single step, a scream pierced the darkness. It was Crystal. And Wishbone knew it wasn't part of the script!

Chapter Three

*C*rystal! Sam jumped up from her seat. A second later the lights were on, and Sam was scrambling up the stairs to the stage. Justin was right behind her.

By the time Sam reached Crystal, Joe, David, and some of the other kids surrounded her. Sam peered through the group.

On the floor, in the middle of the entire cast, sat Crystal. She was holding her right ankle, making a face as if she were in pain.

"What happened?" Sam shouldered her way into the circle of actors and kneeled down beside Crystal.

"Crystal!" Ryan elbowed his way through the other kids and dropped down beside Crystal. "Don't worry. I know some first-aid techniques. Here, let me check out your foot. Can you wiggle your toes?"

"I'll try. . . . Give me a minute, Ryan. It hurts when I move." Crystal held up a pink ponytail scarf. Sam took it and looked at it carefully. Crystal looked puzzled. "When I ran offstage, I slipped on the scarf. I guess I twisted my ankle when I fell."

Slowly, Ryan moved Crystal's foot first in a circle, and then from side to side. "Well, it's definitely not broken, but it seems to be a little swollen. We'd better put ice on it right away."

Sam glanced up at McKenzie as Ryan gently took off Crystal's shoe. McKenzie was looking pretty icy herself.

Wishbone moved closer and he sniffed the scarf dangling from Sam's hand.

Justin pointed at the scarf. "Didn't Rachel bring the scarves today?"

"How'd it get on the stage floor?" Sam frowned.

"Don't look at me!" Rachel's freckled face turned as pink as the scarf.

"Maybe you dropped one and didn't notice," Ryan said.

Rachel shook her head. "I clearly remember putting all the scarves in the wardrobe closet."

Ryan quickly turned his attention back to Crystal. "I think you should go home and put your foot up. You need to R.I.C.E. it. That's what we called it in the first-aid course. **R** is for rest, **I** is for ice, **C** is for . . . I forgot the rest of it." Ryan grinned sheepishly.

Sam had to laugh. Ryan never could remember his lines from the play, either. Still, he sure was making Crystal feel better. "Can you stand up, Crystal?" Sam asked.

Crystal struggled to get up, leaning on Ryan's shoulder.

For a second, Crystal stood there with all her weight on her left foot.

The kids stepped back to give Crystal room.

Crystal took a deep breath. She put her right foot down, then quickly hobbled onto her left one. She took a few more slow steps, limping each time when she put weight on her right foot. Tears glistened in her eyes.

Ryan hurried over and grabbed a chair off the stack near the control panel. He brought it back and helped her sit down.

Murmurs drifted across the stage. "You'll be okay for the show, won't you, Crystal?" Robin Santia asked anxiously. Robin played Sandy's friend, Frenchie. "We can't have *Grease* without Sandy!"

Sam saw the other kids looking from Crystal . . . to her . . . to Justin, hoping for an answer. Sam wished she had one.

Only Justin seemed unshaken by the situation. "Crystal, do you think your ankle will be okay by opening night?"

"Of course I'll be able to perform!" Crystal said, a bit annoyed. "I think I just twisted it a little. I'll be all right if I rest it."

"Okay." Justin nodded quickly and turned away from her. "Amanda, you can take over Crystal's role during rehearsals. That way, if she can't go on opening night, you can—"

"I'd be happy to!" Amanda said excitedly. Immediately, she pulled a rubber band out of one of her pockets and put her hair up in a ponytail, just the way Sandy wore her hair in *Grease*.

Amanda really wanted that part, Sam thought. *Now it looks like she's going to get it, and she can't pretend she's not thrilled.*

Justin ran a hand through his hair and didn't seem to notice Amanda's glee. "I'm glad you can step in for Crystal during rehearsals."

"I'll do anything I need to—to help the play." Amanda's smile was even bigger than before.

Sam saw a flicker of pain on Crystal's face. She wasn't sure if it was caused by her ankle, or by Amanda's enthusiasm. A second later the look was gone, and Sam wondered if she'd seen it at all.

This is awful! Sam thought. First Crystal worries about someone falling and getting hurt. And then she herself slips and gets hurt.

"Hey!" Rachel said, tugging the scarf from Sam's grasp. "Look at this! Someone poked holes through the scarf. It wasn't like this when I brought it to school."

Ryan snatched the scarf away from Rachel. After giving it a quick look, he scrunched it into a ball and handed it back to Rachel. "It could have happened when Crystal slipped on it."

Sam studied Ryan. *Why did he personally examine the scarf?* Her attention was then drawn to McKenzie. She was glaring at Ryan again.

Rachel folded the scarf. "I'll put it back in the wardrobe closet, where it belongs."

Everyone looked at Crystal, and Ryan gave her special attention.

"Do you want to go home?" Ryan asked her. "I can call your parents and wait with you out front."

Crystal hesitated.

"You need to get home and put some ice on your ankle," Sam said.

Ryan smiled at Crystal. "I can carry your books and your coat. Or you can carry mine," he teased, when she still didn't answer.

Ryan was always nice to everyone, but he seemed really eager for Crystal to get home without having any more problems.

He's acting strange . . . different, Sam thought. *Could he be blaming himself? But he had nothing to do with it.*

"I'm trying to decide whether I should walk

36

home. I live really close by. But I suppose I shouldn't try to walk on my foot. I'll call my mom and ask her to pick me up."

"I'll do that." Ryan turned and borrowed a pencil from Justin. "I'll call your mother. What's your phone number, Crystal?" he asked, giving McKenzie a quick glance.

From the look on McKenzie's face, Sam thought she wasn't happy about Ryan's question.

Just then, Rachel burst through the curtained doorway that led from the halls behind the stage. "Look, everyone! I found this on the floor by the wardrobe closet, where the costumes and props are kept." She held up a canvas tennis shoe.

Sam and the others leaned in to get a closer look at the shoe. The shoe was part of a costume. One end of the lace had been completely chewed off. And the canvas heel of the shoe had been chewed ragged. "And a glove from one of the costumes is missing."

Suddenly, all eyes were on Wishbone.

"Helllooo!" Wishbone looked up at the kids. "What's everybody staring at me for? In case you haven't noticed, *my* paws look too good to hide inside a pair of gloves . . . uh, make that *two* pairs of gloves."

"You don't think Wishbone did this, do you?" Sam asked the group.

"You tell 'em, Sam!" Wishbone trotted over to her side.

"Well . . ." Rachel raised her eyebrows. "This

tennis shoe was definitely chewed by something with sharp, pointed teeth. And I'll bet the holes in the scarf were made by teeth, too."

"But I'm not that kind of dog!" Wishbone sat down low on the floor.

Joe reached down and gave Wishbone a scratch behind his brown ear. "He hasn't chewed anything like that since he was a pup."

"Thank you, Joe." Wishbone sat taller. But looking at all the faces above him, Wishbone wasn't sure how many kids Joe had convinced. "If you'll excuse me, there are some ginger snaps in the hall with my name on them."

Wishbone trotted between Joe and David. Then he went through the curtained doorway. Turning right, he trotted down the hall. When he got near the wardrobe closet and saw his dish, he sucked in his breath. The ginger snaps Joe had put out for him were gone!

Wishbone put his nose to the floor and sniffed the area around his dish. "They were here, all right. And so was some dog!" Wishbone sniffed again. "I'll bet it's the same dog that got hold of that scarf and tennis shoe!"

Wishbone checked the area once more for any sign of his ginger snaps.

"Hey, Joe!" Wishbone barked. "Somebody ate my ginger snaps. Could you grab a few more from the box?"

Joe poked his head through the doorway, saw Wishbone, and walked toward him. He looked at Wishbone's food dish. "Quiet, Wishbone. That's all you get to eat for now."

"But, Joe, that's just the point." Wishbone looked up into his pal's eyes. "I didn't get *anything* to eat!"

As Sam and David came up behind Joe, he bent over and picked up a piece of a wrapper. "Hey," he said. "This is from one of those new, crunchy energy bars—just like the one I have in my jacket pocket." Joe disappeared into the dressing room.

"Uh-oh." Wishbone wagged his tail. "Whatever it is, I didn't do it. Honest!"

Joe returned a minute later with another piece of wrapper in his hand. "Wishbone! How can you want more ginger snaps when you ate *my* snack, too?"

Wishbone lay down and put his head on his paws. "Joe. You're not listening."

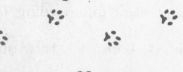

That evening, Sam sat on the couch in her living room and finished the last of her homework. Then she closed her history book and put it on the coffee table.

"Finished?" asked Walter Kepler, Sam's dad. He smiled and sat down in the living room chair with his newspaper.

"Yes, finally," Sam said, sighing. "The play takes up so much of my time. My job was tough enough to begin with, but the closer opening night gets, the more there is that goes wrong."

Her dad raised his eyebrows. "It sounds like you've had one of those days most people would like to forget."

"It's worse than that, Dad. Today, one of our two lead actors, Crystal, showed up late at rehearsal." Sam looked down. "And it might have been my fault. She said I told her the wrong time. I can't remember if I did or not. Then Crystal slipped and hurt her ankle and had to drop out of rehearsal. We don't know if she'll be okay by Friday night."

Walter slipped his reading glasses on and looked at her over the top of them. "Putting on your own show is a very big responsibility, Sam. But I'm sure that you can handle it."

"Thanks, Dad." Sam smiled and picked up *Sleeping Murder,* by Agatha Christie, from the coffee table. "I've been looking forward to reading this all afternoon."

Walter lay his unopened paper in his lap and looked at the book's cover. "Agatha Christie. You, Joe, and David are really into reading mysteries these days."

"Actually, I borrowed this one from Miss

Gilmore," Sam said. "She's a big fan of Miss Marple. Miss Marple is sort of a prim and proper British granny type. But"—Sam held up a finger—"she has twinkling blue eyes that don't miss a thing. And . . . this is the cool part, Dad," Sam said. "She loves to solve crimes. She has this sort of natural instinct she uses."

"A lot of people are fans of Miss Marple," her dad said. "She's famous for her sharp eyes *and* her sharp wit."

Sam nodded in agreement. "In *Sleeping Murder,* a young woman named Gwenda is visiting England and is really fascinated by this old house near the sea. So she buys it. After she moves in, she starts to imagine things about the house. She thinks there's a door where there isn't one . . . a walkway in a different spot. . . . She begins to think the house is haunted." Sam raised her eyebrows. "But the events get even stranger. It turns out the things she's been imagining really used to be like that a long time ago."

"Wow! You've got me hooked, Sam."

Sam smiled. "Me, too."

As Sam opened the book to her bookmark, the last thing she heard was the rustle of her dad's newspaper. By then Sam was already caught up in *Sleeping Murder.* Gwenda, Miss Marple, and some friends had gone to the theater to see a play. When one of the actors delivered a line about dying young, Gwenda screamed. She jumped up and ran out of the theater. Later, Gwenda told Miss Marple she had been frightened because of a vision that had suddenly come to her—a dead body at the bottom of her staircase—a long, long time ago. But Gwenda had never been to England before. If her vision was real, how could she have known about the staircase and the body?

But Miss Marple suspected that Gwenda *had* been to England before, when she was a child. She was right. Now Gwenda's return to England had awakened a "sleeping murder," as Miss Marple called it. It was a murder that happened a long time ago, but it wasn't discovered until Gwenda's vision and the questions that followed. Miss Marple was afraid the murderer might try to kill again—to silence Gwenda.

Sam closed the book and stretched. *Wow!* She thought about the feeling Gwenda got when she heard the actor say his line about dying young. Sam had gotten some strange feelings herself that day. The first time was when McKenzie gave Ryan a look for flubbing his line. The second time involved Ryan, too! It was when he seemed so interested in the scarf. Sam stood up. Unlike Gwenda, Sam hoped she really *was* imagining things.

Her dad had gone into his garage office. The garage had been converted into an office several years before. Sam poked her head into the doorway. "I'm going to bed, Dad."

"Good night, Sam."

"Good night, Dad." As Sam made her way down the hall to her bedroom, she found herself wishing she had time to read another chapter of the book.

Chapter Four

On Tuesday morning Sam woke up a half hour earlier than usual. *I guess it's the excitement of finally seeing David's sign,* she thought. She and Joe were going to meet David in the auditorium before school and help him hang it. Sam smiled. David's sign was just what was needed. It would help put Crystal's accident behind them, and give everyone something fun to focus on.

After Sam got all ready for school, she still had plenty of time before she had to meet the boys. She set the kitchen timer for fifteen minutes. Then she picked up *Sleeping Murder* and began to read at the kitchen table. . . .

Bzzzzzzzz! The fifteen minutes had passed so quickly! Sam jumped up and turned off the kitchen timer. Walking back slowly to the table, she thought, *Gwenda now knows that the dead woman she pictured lying at the bottom of the stairs was her stepmother, Helen. But Helen's brother, Dr. Kennedy, disagrees. He thinks Helen ran away. He even has a letter from her that proves she's still alive.*

Sam put on her jacket and grabbed her history book from the coffee table. *Could Gwenda's vision be something she actually saw happen? If so, why would her memory of what happened to Helen be so different from Dr. Kennedy's version?* Sam was puzzled. *Miss Marple thinks there's a piece of the puzzle still missing. She calls the missing piece "X"— the unknown factor. When Miss Marple finds the missing piece, she'll be able to see the whole picture clearly.*

After locking the front door behind her, Sam walked toward Sequoyah Middle School. The sun was out, and it was another warmer than normal winter day.

From the excitement of Miss Marple's world . . . to the excitement of my own, Sam thought. Her mind returned to the "Greased Lightning" sign. David had a certain knack when it came to creating any kind of special effect.

As Sam got near Oakdale City Hall, a bicycle whizzed up beside her, then slowed.

"Hi, Sam," Damont Jones said. His letterman's jacket was hanging open, and he wore sunglasses. His short brown hair was hidden under a safety helmet.

"Hi, Damont. Are you coming to the play Friday night?" Sam asked.

"Like there's even going to *be* a play." Damont laughed. "I heard about what happened to Crystal. You guys are never going to be able to pull this off without your female star. Don't feel bad, Sam. If there's no play, you can always rent the video of *Grease* and watch it at home."

"No, thanks. I'll be busy backstage on opening night," Sam answered. *I hope,* she added to herself. *Wow! Bad news travels fast.*

Damont gave her a brief nod, then pedaled ahead.

"See you at the play!" Sam called. His comments hurt, but she would not let Damont discourage her. She just knew things would work out.

As Sam got near the school, she saw Joe and Wishbone walking toward her from the opposite direction. "Wait up!" she called. Her steps quickened so that she reached Sequoyah at the same time Joe and Wishbone did. "Hi, Joe." Cradling her book in one arm, she bent down to give Wishbone a quick scratch. "Hi, boy. How's it going?" After patting his side, she stood up. "Come on, Joe."

Sam and Joe cut across the lawn and walked around to the back of the school. Mr. Barnes's car was parked by the backstage door, which had been latched open. Mr. Barnes and David were slowly and carefully lifting David's "Greased Lightning" sign out of the trunk. Sam wasn't surprised to see the front of the sign completely covered with brown construction paper.

"Would you like me to take it from here, Mr. Barnes?" Joe asked.

"That'd be great, Joe." Mr. Barnes released his end of the sign into Joe's hands. As the boys started to make their way through the doorway, Mr. Barnes turned to Sam. "I understand you kids are doing the play without a drama coach this year."

"That's right," Sam said.

"That's a pretty big undertaking." Mr. Barnes smiled encouragingly at Sam. "David said there's been a few accidents—parts of costumes missing . . . that kind of stuff." He glanced at the doorway. "But it seems to me that you're doing a great job, Sam."

Sam hesitated a moment. "I sure hope so."

Mr. Barnes walked back to his car and shut the trunk. Sam walked with him.

"You know, Sam, if we take things as they come, and do our best, things usually work out just fine."

Walking around the car, Mr. Barnes opened the driver's-side door and slid in. "I'm sure with your determination behind it, *Grease* will be a huge success."

Finally, Sam smiled. "Thank you, Mr. Barnes." Waving, she watched him drive off. Then she headed for the backstage door.

Joe was standing just inside the doorway. Wishbone had joined him. "Sorry, boy, it's too early for you to come in now," Joe said. "Come back when it's time for rehearsal—*without* a craving for energy bars."

"Oh, look at his face, Joe," Sam said. "I think you hurt his feelings. I bet he didn't eat your energy bar."

Wishbone barked and wagged his tail.

Joe still didn't seem convinced. "Then who did?"

Shrugging, Sam reached down and unlatched the large hook from the eye that held the door open. When it was nearly shut, Ryan and McKenzie hurried across the lawn behind the school.

"Wait!" Ryan called.

Sam held the door open since there wasn't any outside handle on the stage door.

"Thanks, Sam," McKenzie said, as she and Ryan

headed through the curtained doorway toward the stage area. Sam waited for the door to shut completely. Then she went to meet the others.

Someone had gotten the ladder out of the storage room. It stood on the stage, near the front. Halfway up the ladder was David. He held the top of his still-covered sign with one hand, while the bottom rested on his knee. Joe stood at the foot of the ladder.

Sam walked over and stood next to Joe. She looked around. Amanda was back on the bleachers, practicing her dance steps. *She is really into this!* Sam thought. Justin was onstage, too, standing with Ryan and McKenzie. They were looking at the sign.

David took another step up the ladder. Joe, reaching up, helped steady the sign.

"Maybe I should help also," Justin said.

"That's okay. Joe helped me up to this point. We can manage." Slowly and carefully, David took another step up the ladder.

"Is there something else you need me to do?" Joe asked.

David gently shook his head. "In a minute." Balancing the sign on one knee, David carefully hooked one of the cables dangling from the stage's ceiling to a clip on the back side of the sign. Then he hooked another cable to the clip at the opposite end of the sign. Grabbing one of the hanging electrical cords, he plugged it into the outlet on the back of the sign, near the top.

"Joe, will you go to the control panel and raise the sign with the pulley?"

"I'll do it," Justin said. Joe had already started to

47

walk toward the panel that controlled the stage curtain and the overhead cables. Hesitating, Justin looked up. "David, aren't you going to take the paper off first?"

Joe continued to move toward the panel. David shook his head at Justin. "You can't see it until rehearsal."

Sam smiled and then shrugged her shoulders. "He keeps all his projects a secret until the very last second."

As the sign began to rise, David climbed to the top step of the ladder. He kept his hand on the bottom edge of the sign. "Okay, stop," David called when the sign was hidden up with all the wires, behind the curtain. "Mark that position on the pulley rope as *Sign Up*," he told Joe. "Then bring it down a bit." When the sign hung where the audience would be able to see it, David called, "Okay—there! That's *Sign Down*."

David climbed partway down the ladder. Then he jumped to the stage floor. A thud echoed across the nearly empty stage, as he hit the wood planks.

Justin stepped to the very front edge of the stage and stared up at the brown paper. Sam thought it looked as if he were studying the sign. She wondered what big ideas he had in store for it now.

"Hi, everyone," Crystal said, as she limped through the auditorium door, carrying her schoolbooks. "Is that David's sign?"

"Crystal!" Sam was surprised to see her. "How's your ankle?" She walked to the front edge of the stage. When Crystal sat down in the first row, Sam saw that her ankle was wrapped in an elastic bandage.

Crystal looked up at Sam. "I went to the doctor,

and he said my muscle's having a spasm. I'm supposed to stay off of it as much as possible for a few days."

Crystal winced a little bit and looked down at her foot. Then she seemed to brighten and gave Sam a smile.

"Don't worry," Crystal said. "You'll have the real Sandy onstage opening night!"

Looking around, Crystal spotted Ryan talking to his girlfriend, McKenzie.

"Could somebody help me onstage so I can see the sign, too?" Crystal asked.

Justin answered her. "You can't see it until this afternoon."

Sam watched him walk away. She knew Justin really wanted to see David's sign. Yet he didn't say a word when David announced it wouldn't be unveiled until rehearsal. *He has so much self-control. How does he do it?*

Sam glanced at McKenzie. She wasn't quite so good at hiding her feelings. McKenzie's face had turned bright red when Crystal had asked for help. It was still bright pink as she and Ryan walked toward Sam, arguing.

Crystal sighed from her seat as she watched Amanda dancing on the bleachers. "I guess she's a better dancer than I am."

"Crystal, you're a *great* dancer." Ryan grabbed hold of McKenzie's hand, then smiled down at Crystal.

"He's right," Sam said, trying to cheer her up. "But right now you have to let your ankle heal."

Sam glanced at the clock on the back wall of the auditorium. "Oh, my gosh! It's almost time for first period. I'd better get to my locker." Sam hurried down the stairs and out of the auditorium.

All of the other kids made their way to class.

Tuesday afternoon, Wishbone left his doggie buddies at Jackson Park and trotted over to Joe's school. He stood right beside the big double doors out front. He put his nose to the crack, waiting to run inside the second either door opened.

Wishbone wagged his tail. "I hear the footsteps . . . feel the vibrations . . ." A door burst open, and a boy with big feet ran out. "I see my chance!" Wishbone bolted inside.

"Hi, people!" Wishbone immediately stepped up close to the wall in the school's front hallway. He had learned early on that that was the only way to avoid being stepped on. In another few minutes, the halls would empty out and the whole place would be his! He'd have his very own crumb smorgasbord! Chips, cookie crumbs, candy—the selection changed every day. But he had to get to the crumbs before the custodian cleaned the halls. All he had to do was put his amazing black nose to the floor and sniff!

Wishbone found safety beneath a glass case that held a fire extinguisher.

"'Bye," he said, as kids passed him in a blur of jackets, coats, books, and shoes. "'Bye. See you tomorrow. Be careful crossing the street. Watch out for cats."

When the hall was almost empty, Wishbone put

his nose to the floor. He took the long route to the auditorium. He enjoyed a fine selection of crumbs—choosing only the best.

"At least out here I don't get falsely accused of eating someone's energy bar!"

The dog happened to reach the auditorium at the same time Ryan and McKenzie did. Not only did they look alike, but they were both wearing yellow shirts.

"Hey! It's the double-vision duo!" Wishbone said. He sniffed the air. "*What?* No cookies?"

McKenzie frowned at Ryan. Then she pulled her hand away when he reached for it.

"Helllooo! Things seem a bit chilly between the two of you. And, hey! I'm too young for frostbite." Wishbone wagged his tail. "Door, please."

Ryan opened one of the auditorium doors.

"Thank you," Wishbone said. He bolted inside before either of the kids made a move. Then he trotted forward. "Hey! what's going on?" Instead of being *on*stage, the kids had gathered down in front of it. "Oh! That's right! David brought his sign today."

Wishbone trotted up to the front row, jumped up into one of the seats, and sat down. Looking around, he realized everyone was already there—the entire cast and crew, even Crystal. David was in the wings over at stage right.

"I'm here now, David. You can start."

He tried to wag his tail, but it thumped against the back of the seat.

"Joe! Joe!" he called toward the small group of kids that included Joe. "Over here! I saved you a great seat!"

Joe didn't seem to hear him.

David stepped forward and looked at everyone. "I'm going to close the stage curtain so you'll get the full effect when the sign appears." Turning on his heel, he headed toward the control panel.

The red curtain started to close. Some of the kids took seats, while others stood off to the side.

"Sam! Sam!" Wishbone whispered as Sam sat down next to him. "Do we get popcorn?"

Sam was talking to Crystal, who was sitting on the other side of her. "I can't believe you came to rehearsal. Is it okay for you to be doing so much walking around?"

Crystal shrugged one shoulder. "My ankle still hurts, but I wanted to support you guys," Crystal replied.

Suddenly the auditorium lights went out. "Ugh!" Wishbone gasped. Then, when everyone quieted, the stage curtain slowly started to open. "Oh, this is so exciting!" Wishbone's tail thumped against the back of his seat.

When the curtain was about a third of the way open, a dim light shone from the wings, making the stage glow. The bottom of David's sign slowly lowered below the short strip of curtain that went across the top of the stage. An assortment of *oohs*, *ahs*, and *wows* floated through the room. Small white lights, evenly spaced, lit the bottom of the sign.

Wishbone didn't take his eyes from the stage. The more the curtain opened, the more David's sign lowered. "It's a . . . it's a . . . car!" Wishbone said with excitement when he saw enough of the sign to recognize car tires. "And it's not just any car," Wishbone said. "It's a hot rod! Really sporty-looking. Check out how wide the white walls are on those tires!"

The dog stood on all fours, barely able to control himself.

"They're antique tires—like from the 1950s!" The sign was almost completely visible by then. "That's Greased Lightning!" Wishbone barked excitedly.

Bold, black lightning bolts, outlined in red, ran along the side of the silvery car. More ran up the hood. Small white lights outlined the entire car.

"Now, that's a car worth chasing!"

The *oohs* and *ahs* got louder. Some of the kids stood up to get a better look. Some went up onstage. David stood onstage, too, to get a good look at the sign.

"This is the prime cut of cars, David," Wishbone said, as he trotted up the stairs to the stage. "No bones about it, pal." At the top of the stage steps, Wishbone stopped and stared at the car. "David! The

hood ornament is . . . a dog! Is it me? Is it? Is it? Is it? Hey! Look, everybody!" Wishbone trotted from kid to kid, trying to get someone's attention. "That's me up front on the hood!"

Suddenly the headlights on the car came on. "Cool!" Ryan said.

David walked into the wings again. "Okay, everybody, now watch this," he called out.

A 1950s rock-and-roll song started to play. The headlights on Greased Lightning began flashing and fading—in time with the music!

"It's alive!" Wishbone crept closer. "The nose on the dog doesn't light up or anything, does it, David?" Wishbone sniffed. "Speaking of noses . . . what's that funny smell?"

The fur on the dog's neck stood up. Wishbone ran to the back side of the stage, behind David's sign. In the darkness, Wishbone could see that something up there in the sign was beginning to smolder. Wishbone started to bark loudly.

"Over here—quick! Shut off your sign, David! Take the key out, or do whatever you do to turn it off!"

"Settle down, Wishbone!" As Joe walked over toward Wishbone, the boy sniffed and made a face. "Something back here smells weird."

Wishbone kept barking. "That's what I've been trying—"

A puff of smoke rose from the back of the sign. Sparks shot out from the sign's electrical unit, then rained down on the stage. In a thunder of footsteps, the kids scattered.

Chapter Five

Sam held up her hand to shield her face from the sparks shooting out of David's sign. At her feet, Wishbone continued to bark out a warning.

Sam was bumped from the side. As she struggled to keep her balance, she glimpsed dark hair and a flash of yellow. Suddenly the lights on the sign crackled like fireworks. She heard an even louder *pop*. A second later, a white flash followed, forcing her to shut her eyes against the glare. Then the sign went dark.

Sam opened her eyes. In the dim glow of light coming from the wings, she saw David. His hand flew across the control panel on the wall, flipping switches to Off. Then he put a hand on his sound system, and the music stopped.

The auditorium lights brightened. Sam saw Joe standing by David. "Is everyone okay?" she asked, her heart pounding.

David nodded, then stared at his sign.

Sam did a head check of the others. Wishbone

and Justin were onstage with Sam. Ryan and McKenzie were halfway to the auditorium doors. Everyone but Justin looked a little pale.

"Cool effect, David," Ryan said. "Was that supposed to happen?"

"What *did* happen, David?" Justin's tone was very serious.

"Yeah," the other kids chimed in, as they walked cautiously back toward the stage.

David stepped closer to the spot where the accident had occurred and looked up, baffled. "I don't know. When I tried the system out at home last night, it worked perfectly. I'll trip the circuit breaker to cut the power off, then bring the sign down." David walked over to the electrical box and flipped switches.

"You should have listened to my ideas about the sign, David," Justin said. "At least the fireworks would have been *planned*."

David glanced over his shoulder at Justin. By the look on David's face, Sam knew he disagreed.

"Justin, David carefully plans his projects. Something just went wrong. I'll go get the ladder," Joe said. He went through the curtained doorway to head to the storage room. Wishbone followed him.

Sam let her eyes roam over the front of the sign. From what she could see, it looked perfectly normal.

When Joe came back out to the stage area, he set the ladder beneath the sign.

After dragging the ladder a few inches to the left, David climbed up the rungs and unhooked his sign.

Sam and Joe reached up to help steady it.

"Careful," David said. "Got it?"

"Got it," Joe said, as he and Sam lowered the sign. Then they took it to the back of the stage and leaned it against the bleachers. The back side was facing out.

David went into the wings and turned on more stage lights. Then he came out onstage and kneeled down in front of the sign.

Leaning over David's shoulder, Sam checked out the back of the sign, too. It was made from plywood. A green electrical cord was taped flat against the wood. Close to the top of the sign, a few inches below the electrical plug, was a black smudge. Sam frowned. *What's that?* she wondered.

The rest of the kids gathered closer as David examined the plug and cord.

Joe pointed to the black mark at the top of the sign. "It looks like the wood's burned."

Frowning, David sat back on his heels.

Sam tried to think of an explanation. "Maybe your string of lights was faulty, or it was ready to burn out."

David shook his head. "I don't think so, Sam." He pointed to a spot on each of the three electrical wires that were woven together. The green coating was melted away. "It looks like the insulation might've gotten cut on all three of the wires. When I turned on the sign, the exposed wires touched and caused a short. That caused the problem."

Squatting down next to David, Justin leaned in for a better look. "Didn't I see the sign hanging out of your dad's trunk? Maybe the trunk lid cut the cord."

Amanda looked disappointed. "Can't you just fix it? I want to rehearse." Her feet moved rhythmically as she went back to practicing one of her dance steps.

A worried look crossed Crystal's face. "But if this happens during the performance, someone could get hurt."

"It won't," David assured her. "Something is wrong here." He looked at Justin. "My dad and I had the sign wrapped in foam rubber—even the part that was sticking out of the trunk. And he drove really slow." David stared off in thought. "This morning after the sign was hung, I put the ladder back in the storage room." His eyebrows scrunched together. "But when I got here this afternoon, it was out here again. I returned it *again* to the storage room before all of you arrived this afternoon."

Justin stood up. "Well, whatever happened to the sign, you'll just have to fix it. Let's start rehearsal."

Sam watched Justin walk away. *No matter what happens, Justin is always acting as if it's "business as usual,"* she thought. *But something doesn't make sense here. How could a sign that worked fine last night suddenly start to smoke and throw off sparks?* Sam couldn't help but think of Miss Marple's X—the missing piece of the puzzle. Sam was definitely missing a piece to her own puzzle.

In the evening darkness, Wishbone sniffed the grass and bushes along one side of the Oakdale train station, as he continued his investigation. He was determined to find the ginger-snap thief. That hound chewed on everything in his path—ginger snaps, Joe's energy bar, the ponytail scarf, and the tennis shoe. But remembering David's sign, Wishbone had even more to worry about. "Dogs do not climb ladders. We have *two* stage invaders on the loose!"

As he started toward the other side of the train station, a gentle wind ruffled his coat. He sniffed a bush.

"Hmm . . ." said the Jack Russell terrier. "Recent canine visitors have been Bruno and Sparkey, though I'd bet my next soup bone the two didn't come together." He moved his nose along the grass to the gravel to the railroad tracks. "I've sniffed half of Oakdale. There's nothing even close to the scent that the ginger-snap thief left next to my bowl."

Wishbone sat down to scratch his neck. A sudden gust of wind blew at his back. Another gust, a stronger one, followed immediately. Wishbone watched a crumpled piece of paper blow down the street.

"Want to race, huh?" He barked and chased the ball of paper. "You can't outrun Super Dog!"

Wishbone caught up to the paper and ran alongside it.

"I'm faster than a speeding train, able to leap railroad tracks in a single—" Wishbone leaped. "Well . . . okay, make that *two* bounds," he said, taking another leap. Just when he had almost reached the ball of paper again, the wind whisked it into the sky. "And that is *out* of bounds."

Wishbone sniffed the air.

"My trusty nose tells me there's a storm coming." Just then, the hide on his back tightened, and the fur on his neck bristled. "And it's close!"

Tucking his ears low to keep the wind out, Wishbone put his nose to the ground and quickly continued his search for the ginger-snap thief. The wind was blowing so hard that his detecting mission was getting difficult. As soon as he found one scent, the wind blew ten more his way.

Wishbone worked his way toward Sequoyah Middle School. "Nothing . . . nothing . . . nothing," he said, his nose working constantly across the grass. When he reached the back side of the school, he was protected a bit from the wind. "Cat," he said, sniffing a patch of dirt. He continued on. "More cat." He stopped at a bush. "Bingo! New dog scent!"

Chapter Six

Sam stood behind the preparation counter at Pepper Pete's Pizza Parlor, the restaurant her dad owned. She added sauce to the two pizza crusts in front of her. Glancing up, she saw a piece of a branch blow by the front window. The TV weather forecaster had predicted a storm. *Pepper Pete's is the perfect place to be right now,* Sam thought. *The heat from the ovens and the smell of melting cheese make it feel warm and cozy.* And she must not be the only one who thought so.

Miss Gilmore and some of her friends from the Arbor Society were sitting at one booth having dinner. A family Sam had seen at the restaurant a few times before was sitting at another booth. Closer, at one of the small tables, sat Ryan and McKenzie. They were sharing a pizza, as any other couple would do. But that was about all they were sharing. Ryan was trying to start up a conversation, but McKenzie answered each question with a flat yes or no.

The door opened. Sam looked up. As Crystal

limped in, a rush of cold air followed her. The breeze temporarily cooled off the restaurant.

When Crystal started to sit at a table all by herself, Ryan smiled at her. "Are you alone?"

She nodded. "Yes."

Leaning sideways, Ryan pulled over a chair from an empty table. "Why don't you sit with us?"

"Thanks." Crystal smiled. "Hi, McKenzie." After removing her coat, Crystal sat down.

"Hi." A frown instantly formed on McKenzie's face.

Sam added cheese and pepperoni to one of the pizzas, then shoved it into the hot oven. Wiping her hands, she walked over to see what Crystal wanted to order.

"Ryan just offered me their last piece of pizza," Crystal said. "Thanks anyway, Sam. I won't be staying long."

Crystal seemed totally unaware of McKenzie's unfriendly glare.

Smiling, Sam hurried over to Miss Gilmore's table. "Can I get you anything else?" she asked cheerfully.

The women shook their heads. "No, thank you, Sam," Miss Gilmore said. "We're doing fine. Oh!" she added excitedly. "How are you doing with *Sleeping Murder?*"

"I'm really into it. Oh, thank you again for letting me borrow your copy. In fact, I was just reading about Miss Marple's theory of X—"

"The unknown factor!" Miss Gilmore cut in. "The missing piece to the puzzle!"

Sam nodded. "When it comes to our school play,

I think I might have an X of my own. Someone seems to be playing pranks at rehearsal."

The phone on the wall near the preparation counter started to ring.

"Excuse me," Sam said. "I'd better get that."

Miss Gilmore wiggled her fingers in the air in a sort of wave. "Good luck finding your missing puzzle piece, Sam!"

"Thanks, Miss Gilmore." As Sam headed to the phone, she noticed Ryan, McKenzie, and Crystal with their heads together. They were talking low and kept glancing at Sam.

Sam wondered why they kept looking at her. As she answered the phone and wrote down a pizza order, Ryan helped Crystal to the front door. With a wave to Sam, she left. Ryan went back and sat down with McKenzie.

Sam added cheese to the crust in front of her and started preparing it to order. A few moments later, Ryan and McKenzie stood at the counter, with their hands placed on top of it. Both had weird looks on their faces, as if they wanted to tell Sam something.

Sam hoped it wasn't more bad news about the play. She stopped working. "What's the matter?"

McKenzie and Ryan exchanged glances. "Crystal told us something," McKenzie said. "It was something she didn't want to tell you about, because she thinks you have enough to deal with already."

"Yeah," Ryan said, his usual smile gone. "But McKenzie and I think you should know."

"What is it?" As Sam glanced from one to the other, her heart skipped a beat.

McKenzie sat on one of the counter stools while Ryan explained. "After what happened to David's sign, Crystal's sure that the play is being sabotaged. In fact, she thinks *she* was the first victim—you know, slipping on the scarf." Ryan sighed and glanced at McKenzie. "We thought you should know, Sam. Crystal thinks someone else in the cast might be targeted to get hurt next."

Sam could hardly believe what she was hearing. *Could Crystal have been set up to fall? Is someone else in danger?*

Wind whipped droplets of rain sideways against the front window.

"Oh, no! It's starting to rain!" McKenzie said.

Ryan shook his head as another gust of wind slammed against the window. "You're wrong—it's starting to *pour.*"

McKenzie pulled Ryan's hand off the counter. "Come on! I'll get my jacket, and we better go before it gets any worse. 'Bye, Sam."

"'Bye." Sam watched the pair prepare to leave. She was still deep in thought about what they'd told her. Finally, a ding from the oven timer brought her back to her job. She quickly finished putting the anchovies on the pizza in front of her, then turned and slid it into the oven. Using a pizza board, she removed the pizza she'd placed in the oven earlier. The cheese had bubbled up in spots and browned perfectly. Sam placed the pizza on a serving pan and stuck it under the warmer.

Ryan opened Pepper Pete's front door. As he and McKenzie ran out into the stormy night, Joe and David hurried inside. Their hair was wet, and rain spots covered their jackets. They headed for the preparation counter.

Sam smiled. "Hi, guys. Maybe you two should do what Wishbone does and give yourselves a good shaking." She handed them the pizza she'd just taken out of the oven.

"Perfect timing!" David said.

"Get a table," Sam said. "I'll tell my dad I'm on my break. Then I'll grab some plates and we can all eat together."

Sam went into the kitchen.

When she came back, she nodded at David as she set the plates down on a table. "Hey, do you know you have a bluish stripe on the left side of your neck?"

David wiped at the line. "We were painting clouds."

Wearing an apron over his clothes, Sam's dad

brought out a tray with three soft drinks on it. "Hi, kids." He set the drinks on their table.

"Thanks, Mr. Kepler," Joe said, picking up his glass.

"My pleasure, Joe." He looked at David. "Sam told me about your sign, David. I'm really sorry."

David nodded. "I can fix it easily enough, as long as I can find another string of those small Christmas lights in my attic." He smiled. "The *good news* for today is that Joe and I just came from school, where we finished painting the last of the scenery props."

"And," Joe added, "we asked the nighttime custodian not to lock us out. This way, we can go back after dinner and move all the props to the stage area."

"That's great. Sam said she'd be helping you tonight." Mr. Kepler glanced out the window. "With the weather the way it is, I doubt if we'll have too many more customers."

"Thanks for the drinks, Dad," Sam said, as he turned and disappeared through the swinging doors into the kitchen.

A gust of wind rattled the windows as if it had heard her dad's words. The kids all looked out through the glass.

"Wow!" David said, picking up another slice of pizza. "Stuff is flying all over. It looks like this is going to be a really nasty storm."

"Maybe we should finish eating quickly and get back to school so we can get home early," Joe said.

"That sounds fine with me," Sam said, as rain pelted the window. She looked at the boys. Taking a deep breath, she told them what Crystal had said to McKenzie and Ryan. "The idea of someone sabotaging the play sort of gives me the creeps," she said when she'd finished.

"Well, after taking a close look at my sign . . ." David hesitated, looking troubled. "I actually think Crystal might be right. I'm positive that my sign was sabotaged."

Sam frowned as she stared at her slice of pizza. "So there really *could* be an X who wants to destroy the production!"

"An X?" Joe asked.

"Oh." Sam realized she hadn't told the boys about X—the unknown, or the book. "X is the missing piece of the puzzle that Miss Marple talks about in the mystery, *Sleeping Murder.* I just started reading the book a few nights ago, and the story really has me hooked. Anyway, the missing piece of the puzzle could be someone's motive. Or it could be some other missing piece of information, or the guilty party."

Sam nibbled a bite from her pizza before she turned the conversation back to the play.

"X *could* be Ryan," she said. "A delay in the opening of the play would certainly be to his advantage. He still doesn't know his lines. And he's been acting sort of weird."

"Yeah," Joe agreed. "Did you see the way he grabbed the scarf from Rachel?"

"He also seems much too concerned about Crystal." Sam wiped her fingers on a napkin. "It's almost as if he might feel guilty about something. But then there's McKenzie. She could be X, too."

"Because she's jealous of the attention Ryan is giving to Crystal?" David guessed.

Shaking her head, Sam stirred her straw in her half-empty glass. "I think it's more than that. I think she's jealous of the attention he's giving to the whole play."

Joe finished off his slice of pizza. "I guess she *has* been giving him the cold shoulder lately."

Sam nodded and stacked Joe's empty plate on top of her own.

"Justin could be X," David said. "I wouldn't let him add his techno stuff to my sign. It's like a competition thing with him. He wanted me to have fire shoot out of Greased Lightning's exhaust pipe." David handed his plate to Sam.

"Now I understand why he was staring at your sign." Sam untied her Pepper Pete's apron and slipped it off over her head. "I'll tell my dad we're leaving."

David and Joe continued to discuss the X factor while they waited for Sam.

Sam carried the tray of dishes into the kitchen and set them down next to the large sink. "I'll be back later, Dad, to catch a ride home."

"Okay, Sam."

Sam walked back out into the hallway leading from the dining room to the kitchen. She grabbed her jacket from a hook on the wall. Then she met the boys at the front door. The three stepped out into the rainy night.

Wishbone followed the new dog scent from the first bush to the second, then toward the back wall of the school. A big drop of rain splattered on his ear. Wishbone's head popped up. Another raindrop hit his muzzle. Suddenly rain pelted him from head to tail.

"Talk about bad timing!" Wishbone sniffed the freshly washed air and grass. "Now everything's one big combination scent—kind of like a Pepper Pete's pizza with everything on it!" He sighed. He'd lost the scent. "So close, yet so far away. Oh, well . . ." Lowering his head against the rain, he trotted toward Pepper Pete's. Wishbone had overheard Sam the day before, telling Joe and David about meeting them at Pepper Pete's.

Through the pouring rain, Wishbone saw the kids come out of the restaurant.

"Joe! Sam! David!" He trotted over to meet them. "It's getting really, really wet out here. Don't you want to go back inside and give the dog some pizza?"

The kids greeted Wishbone. Then they stepped off the curb and into the driving rain.

"Okay, later, then." Wishbone followed them back toward the school. While the kids hurried up the walkway toward the front entrance, Wishbone trotted onto the cold, soggy school lawn. "Oh, that feels good on the paws!"

Lightning lit up the sky.

Wishbone ran to the front doors with the kids. They were standing under the small overhang, which protected them from the rain. "Okay, step aside. Dogs and children first." He shook the rain from his coat.

"Wishbone!" The kids held out their hands as shields against Wishbone's spraying.

"Oops! Sorry. Can we go in now?" Wishbone

wagged his tail. "Before the sky makes that sound like it's cracking open really wide?"

As Joe reached for the door, thunder rumbled, then crashed above them.

"Too late!" Wishbone yelled.

Chapter Seven

When Joe opened one of the school's front doors, he motioned for Sam to go in first.

"Thanks." Remembering her wet shoes, Sam stepped carefully onto the clean, dry floor to keep from slipping. She didn't want to end up with a sprained ankle like Crystal. Wishbone came inside behind her. Then Joe and David followed.

As the door clicked shut behind them, Wishbone trotted ahead.

"Wait, boy," Joe called, turning the other way. "We're going to the art room first."

Four windows—those next to the double doors, and in the top half of each door—lit up from the lightning. The lights flickered. A few seconds later, when the lights still remained on, Sam heard Joe breathe a sigh of relief. Sam shivered, but not because of the flickering lights. She was still worried that someone was trying to sabotage the play. *Who is it?* Sam wondered.

"We'd better hurry," Joe said. "I don't know about you, but I don't want to be stuck in a windowless hallway if the lights go out."

"Right," David agreed.

They all quickened their steps. Even Wishbone. Thunder crashed outside. It was so loud that Sam thought she felt the building shake. She hurried faster. Reaching the art room, Sam hesitated a second before opening the door. She couldn't shake her creepy feeling. *This just isn't like me!* she thought. *Is there an unpleasant surprise waiting for me on the other side of the door?* With a quick glance behind her at the boys, she gathered her courage and pulled open the door.

"Gosh!" she said, surprised. Immediately she felt better. The entire room was filled with free-standing scenery props. Sam stepped inside and did a slow turn. She gazed at the life-sized cardboard jukebox that would be used to set the scene for Hamburger Palace, the place where the Grease kids hung out near their high school. Her eyes roamed to the huge, bluish-white cardboard clouds that would be used for Wishbone's teen-angel scene. "These are *so* cool, guys."

Sam had to smile, thinking of how funny it was going to be to see Wishbone surrounded by clouds, giving heavenly advice to mixed-up Frenchie in a splashy musical number.

"Thanks," Joe said.

While Wishbone checked out a cutout of racing hot rods, Sam's eyes scanned some of the other props. The lights flickered, making her jump. *What's wrong with me tonight?* she wondered.

"We'd better get moving," Sam said. "We have a lot to do."

"I'm with you," Joe said, frowning up at the lights. "I just hope the power doesn't go out before we're finished."

Joe grabbed the jukebox. Sam and David carried clouds.

With Wishbone in the lead, they made their way toward the auditorium. Their footsteps echoed in the empty hall. Sam started to get that creepy feeling again. *This is silly!* Sam thought. *I'm getting jumpy at the sound made by my own feet!*

Opening the auditorium doors, Joe directed Sam and David through. Then he and Wishbone followed them.

The lights flickered, then dimmed. A second later, as the double doors clanked shut behind them, the lights went out. Sam froze. She held her breath for a few seconds. She was paralyzed with fear! Sam squinted into the blackness of the windowless auditorium. Her heartbeat pounded loudly in her ears. Reaching out with one hand, she searched for a row of seats, or a wall. Something solid, familiar. But her hand only sliced through the black, black air and dropped to her side.

As Sam stood there, hoping the lights would come back on soon, she got an even eerier feeling. Her breathing turned heavy, almost drowning out the sound of her heartbeat. Goose bumps shot up her arms. Sam didn't know how she knew, but she knew. Something wasn't right.

"Joe . . . David!" she whispered. "I think some-one else is in here with us!"

The fur on Wishbone's neck bristled. "I *know* someone else is in the auditorium, Sam." Wishbone sensed the kids' uneasiness, especially Sam's. "Helllooo! Come out, come out, wherever you are." He growled to let whoever was in the auditorium with them know that he meant to protect his pack.

Wishbone cocked his head and listened. His excellent canine sense of hearing picked up footsteps on the stairs to the stage.

"Come back here, you coward!" Wishbone called. "Even though the kids can't hear you, *I* can." He looked over his shoulder through the darkness, toward the kids. "No need to panic. I have everything under control. Super Dog can handle any situation. Does anybody have a flashlight?"

Wishbone heard more footsteps, just as soft as before, but moving quicker now. They were going in the direction of a back corner of the stage. Then something *clinked*.

Wishbone worked his way forward, trying to sniff out the culprit. "This auditorium has more scents than a cat has fleas." As he reached the stage steps, he heard the soft *creak* and *click* of the backstage door opening and closing. "Sam!" He barked. "Whoever it is is getting away out the back door. Hurry, guys!"

Suddenly, Wishbone quieted and jerked his head around. A low, low rumbling and heavy footsteps sounded behind the kids, on the other side of the auditorium doors.

"I'm warning you!" Wishbone wagged his tail with concern in the dark. "There's a five-hundred-pound attack dog in here!" The Jack Russell terrier made his way back toward where the kids were.

The auditorium doors slowly opened.

Wishbone heard his human pals' breathing grow shallow and shaky. In a flash, he positioned himself protectively in front of the kids. Then he released a long, low growl.

"Who's here?" A deep voice bellowed at them through the darkness.

Wishbone's heartbeat quickened.

Suddenly the lights flickered, then stayed on.

Sam, Joe, and David all let out a loud sigh of relief.

Wishbone wagged his tail at the custodian, who stood in the doorway with his cleaning cart. "Boy, am I glad to see you! Someone was sneaking around in here, and we need to go after—"

"I *thought* I heard a noise in the hall," the custodian said, motioning behind him. "It must've been you kids moving your stuff over here." He looked at their faces. "Oh. Sorry if I scared you." He bent over and picked a scrap of paper off the floor.

"Like I was saying," Wishbone said. "I heard something drop. Then someone sneaked out, and we need—"

"We're just glad it's you!" Sam glanced at Joe and David, then smiled weakly. "Maybe my imagination was getting the best of me earlier. Maybe the someone I thought I sensed in the auditorium with us was just the custodian coming down the hall."

"No, Sam, it wasn't!" Wishbone put his front

paws on Sam's leg as he tried to convince her. "Believe me, a dog knows these things!"

The lights flickered again. Everyone glanced up. Wishbone immediately sensed the kids' uneasiness.

The custodian shook his head. "I know I told you I'd keep the school open so you could move your things while I clean, but I've changed my mind. With the lights threatening to go out again, I think you might be safer at home."

Joe glanced up at the lights. "I am definitely convinced." He set the cardboard jukebox down in a back corner of the auditorium. "We'll just leave the scenery props here for tonight."

"Yeah," David said, as he and Sam did the same with the clouds.

"No! Wait! You don't understand!" Wishbone insisted, as his friends started to walk out the auditorium doors. "Joe! Sam! David! We need to check out the stage. I think whoever was here dropped a clue!"

"Come on, Wishbone," Joe called, as the lights dimmed slightly.

For a second, Wishbone just stood there looking at them. Then, sighing, he trotted after the kids. "Nobody ever listens to the dog!"

At home, Sam felt much better. Safe. "Good night, Dad," she said, walking into the kitchen. Her dad was sitting at the table, eating ice cream from a carton. The room glowed in candlelight. The rainstorm had blown out the electrical power. "Isn't it a little cold to be eating ice cream?" Sam asked him. She held *Sleeping Murder* in one hand, a flashlight in the other.

Walter Kepler smiled. "With the power out, I was afraid it might melt. You know I wouldn't want it to go to waste," he teased. He nodded at her hands. "I bet you're going to read in bed, like you used to when you were little. Only then you hid under the covers."

"You and Mom knew?" Sam couldn't believe it. All this time she thought it had been her own little secret.

"Well, Sam, at first we didn't." He scooped out another spoonful of ice cream from the carton. "But after replacing dead battery after dead battery in all the flashlights around the house, we finally figured it out. And," he added, "we used to do the same thing ourselves when we were much, much younger."

Laughing, Sam gave her dad a hug. Then she headed to her room, using the flashlight to guide her.

In bed, with the wind pounding against her window and the rain beating on the roof, Sam opened *Sleeping Murder*. She read for a long time. Then she stared out her window into the darkness, thinking about the book.

Miss Marple had learned that for a while Helen lived with her brother, Dr. Kennedy. Helen asked him to put up a tennis net so she'd have something fun to do when her friends came by. But no sooner had Dr. Kennedy put the net up than someone cut it to shreds. Miss Marple called it "a nasty bit of spite." And no one would admit to doing it.

Sam took a deep breath, closed the book, then turned off the flashlight. "Well," she said into the darkness, "somebody's lying . . . but who?"

Chapter Eight

Wishbone's Wednesday afternoon nap ended a little earlier than usual. Yawning, he looked around the Talbots' study. He stretched, then jumped down from his big red chair. "This dog has places to go, people to see, and things to do!"

Trotting down the hall, he disguised his voice to sound like that of a television reporter.

"Today at Sequoyah Middle School, the amazing and handsome dog Wishbone will be rehearsing his Guardian Angel role from the smash-hit *Grease*. People, don't miss this rehearsal. I give this performance two paws up!" Wishbone could feel his excitement building.

Remembering last night, Wishbone hoped the clue he heard drop in the auditorium might still be there . . . if it was a clue.

In the kitchen, he sniffed his dish. "Yum." He chomped down the kibble left from lunch. Then he started for his doggie door. "Uh-oh."

Wishbone stopped, suddenly very aware of his

stomach. Even when he was standing still, it felt as if his stomach was doing flips without him.

"Okay, so I'm a little nervous about performing." Wishbone walked back and forth across the kitchen, trying to make the feeling go away. "Okay . . . so I'm a *lot* nervous." His eyes scanned the room for something that would help calm him. "Coffeepot, refrigerator, newspaper . . ."

As he turned around to walk back the other way, Wishbone lowered his eyes to the floor.

"Water dish, food dish—squeaky book!" Hurrying over to Joe's chair, Wishbone poked his head through the legs. He gently grabbed the yellow toy. "I feel better already."

He trotted happily out his doggie door.

"If Ryan can bring sunglasses to rehearsal to make him *look* better, I can bring squeaky to make me *feel* better."

Wishbone breathed deeply, enjoying the fresh air cleansed by last night's storm. Heading out of the cul-de-sac, he glanced longingly at the yard of his next-door neighbor, Wanda Gilmore.

"Rehearsals have seriously cut down on my digging time. . . ." Suddenly, he raced off toward Wanda's flower bed. "Why not? I still have a few minutes before I have to be at rehearsal." He set squeaky down.

But just as Wishbone's front paws began to scratch the wet dirt, he heard, *"Wishbone!"*

Wishbone turned around in a flash. "Wanda!" He took a small step to the side to hide the fresh markings in the dirt.

Wanda, wearing an orange rain slicker with

matching boots and hat, stood at the side of her house. She held up a small windsock with the end chewed off. "Did you do this, Wishbone?"

Wagging his tail, Wishbone sat down. "No, but thanks for *asking,* Wanda. You'd be surprised how many people automatically *assume* I'm the guilty party."

Hmm . . . Wishbone wasn't sure why, but Wanda continued to hold up the windsock and stare at him. And she didn't even have a small smile on her face.

"Uh . . . maybe I'll come back some other time," he said, picking up squeaky and backing away.

He backed into the underside of a bush. It was almost dry. Wishbone's nose twitched. He was on to something! The scent was very, very faint, but there was no mistaking it. *The ginger-snap thief has been under this bush!*

Wishbone put his nose to the ground and found the dog's trail. The scent seemed to fade away and then come back again. "I'd say the thief was here sometime *after* last night's storm, but before one of today's showers."

But Wishbone knew if he didn't leave right then, he'd be late for rehearsal. For a second, he considered his choices. *Should I stay here and try to catch the ginger-snap thief? Or should I go to rehearsal?*

Wishbone took off. "Sam is depending on me!" With squeaky securely in his mouth, Wishbone raced toward the school. "But I'll be back, you snack-snatcher."

By the time Wishbone reached the auditorium, the stage had already been set up to look like Hamburger Palace, the hangout of the kids in the play.

A table and four chairs were set up. Tall glasses with straws were sitting on the table. Included in the scene were stools and a counter.

At the top of the steps leading up to the stage, Wishbone stopped to catch his breath. "Wow!" Most of the kids were off in the wings, checking out the scenery props. "Isn't it a little crowded in here?"

Wishbone trotted over to Joe, who was sitting on a wooden storage seat by the control panel. He gently dropped squeaky on the floor.

"Great scenery props, buddy."

Without a word, Joe reached down and scratched Wishbone behind the ears.

"Perfect, Joe," Wishbone said, looking up.

While Joe's hand was on Wishbone, the boy's attention was on Sam, David, and Justin. The three were deep in conversation at the end of the counter farthest away from him. They were talking low, but Wishbone heard them, clear as a doorbell.

"Today is the tech rehearsal," Justin said, sticking his pencil behind his ear. "David's sign is supposed to be tested today."

"I'm sorry," David said. "It's not ready. I helped Joe finish up the scenery props last night."

Justin scratched his head, making his curly blond hair stick out on one side.

"It couldn't be helped, Justin," Sam said. "The sign will be ready tomorrow."

Justin looked at his watch, shook his wrist, then looked at his watch again.

Sam glanced at her watch, too. "We'd better get started."

Justin scanned the stage, located Wishbone, and smiled. "We can start with Wishbone's Guardian Angel scene in the Hamburger Palace. Wishbone deserves a turn in the limelight. And we can see if the in-line skates for this scene work okay. Wishbone, are you ready for your scene?"

Wishbone barked.

Without saying another word, Justin walked down the stage steps. He took his usual seat in the front row.

"Robin?" Sam called, glancing around until she spotted her. Robin was playing the role of Frenchie. "Are you ready to start the Guardian Angel scene?"

"Sorry, Sam." Robin went over to another storage seat. Lifting the lid, she pulled out her in-line skates.

"Ready in a jiff," she said, sitting on the floor to remove her shoes.

Wishbone grabbed squeaky in his teeth. Hurrying to the wings at stage left, he released his toy on the floor, then lay down beside it. "I'll be waiting right over here, Sam . . . patiently . . . until my cue to go on. But could you hurry, Sam? I'm really, really, really excited."

"Places, everybody," Sam called, as Joe pulled the lever to close the curtains.

As the house lights went down, Amanda-as-Sandy, Robin-as-Frenchie, and Ryan-as-Danny scrambled to their places. A second later the curtains parted again. The friends in the Hamburger Palace were gathered around a table.

"You know, it really looks like a hamburger place!" Wishbone said. He sniffed. "But you can't fool my nose!"

Danny sat backward in his chair, his arms leaning across the top in a cool way. *Ryan really knows how to be Danny, the top dog of the high school,* Wishbone thought. *Especially when he doesn't have any lines to forget!* Danny's eyes were locked on Sandy, who sat across from him. She was playing hard-to-get, ignoring his too-cool attitude.

They were both pretending not to like each other instead of saying how they really felt. Robin, who was playing their other friend, Frenchie, kept adjusting the scarf on her head—like maybe she had a flea problem. She was really covering up a big problem she didn't want anyone to know about.

Robin sighed, dropping into character as

Frenchie. "I'm really in trouble, guys," she said to Sandy and Danny. "I dropped out of high school to go to beauty school. But it's a lot harder than I thought. I even failed tinting class. Look." She slid the scarf she was wearing on her head to her shoulders.

"Whoa! Pink hair!" Danny whistled.

In the wings beside Wishbone, Rachel-as-Rizzo was getting ready to go onstage. That meant it was almost time for his scene. He was so excited, he gave his squeaky book a little bite.

Rachel ran into the Hamburger Palace. "Come on, everybody!" she called. "Drag races!" As she ran off-stage, everyone in the Hamburger Palace—except Robin—ran after her. The kids ended up offstage near Wishbone.

"Great job, everyone!" he said.

Back onstage, Frenchie stirred her empty glass with her straw. She gave a deep sigh. "I wish I had a Guardian Angel to tell me what to do."

"That's my cue!" Wishbone said. The lights dimmed low for his entrance.

Wishbone flipped. "It's my turn!" He wagged his tail as the stage crew hurried to set out the cloud scenery props. A big, fluffy cloud was rolled out of the wings, and the front of the stage was lined with smaller clouds. Wishbone got ready to run.

When the last crew member left the stage, Wishbone ran out and bounded up the hidden steps to the top of his cloud. He was several feet off the ground. Sitting on a white pillow on top of the prop, Wishbone knew he looked just like a Guardian Angel.

David's cassette tape started playing a song, and

the spotlight focused on Wishbone. Frenchie gasped when she saw her own Guardian Angel looking down at her. Then she glided over to him on skates that were hidden by the clouds at the edge of the stage.

Wishbone prepared to wow everyone with his number. The tape began to play the song "Beauty School Dropout."

Suddenly, Wishbone cocked his head. He thought he heard a noise. *What is that?* he wondered, as the tape continued. He pawed the air as Frenchie skated a circle around the stage.

Now Wishbone *knew* he heard a noise—a low, rhythmic *whump*. Immediately he sensed danger. He pricked up his ears. The sound was coming from one of Robin's skates! The faster she went, the closer together the *whumps* got. And it looked as if she was struggling to turn one skate. *Whumpwhumpwhump.*

"Robin!" Wishbone barked.

Robin circled the stage again. She was starting to

look scared. Leaning, but unable to turn, Robin raced wide-eyed, out of control, toward the edge of the stage.

"Robin!" Leaping from his cloud, Wishbone ran after her, barking, nipping at her heels.

As Robin's head snapped around to look at him, she completely lost her balance. Her arms flew up, and her feet flew out from under her. She toppled over.

Wishbone stood over her. "Speak to me, Robin. Are you okay?"

Chapter Nine

"Robin!" Sam flew up the stage steps, her heart pounding.

Robin was sitting on the floor, rubbing her elbow. Ryan was kneeling beside her. Wishbone stayed close to Robin's side, like a guard.

"What happened? Are you okay?" Sam asked. *This can't be happening again!* she thought, as Justin hurried to her side.

"I think so," Robin said, as McKenzie and Amanda came out of the wings. She looked at her arm. "I think I just skinned my elbow. But that was really scary!"

Standing on the auditorium floor just below the front of the stage was Crystal. "It looked like the dog scared Robin and made her fall." She winced. "He's such a cute little guy, I hate to say this. But maybe he should be kept on a leash from now on."

"You're kidding!" Sam said, as Joe, David, and the others gathered around them.

Unbuckling her skates, Robin said, "Wishbone

didn't scare me—I was already scared. For some reason, when I started going really fast, I couldn't turn my skates. I just kept zipping toward the edge of the stage. Then my mind went blank—I didn't know what to do." Robin looked at Crystal. "So, yes, his barking startled me and made me fall." Robin reached over and scratched Wishbone under his chin. "But Wishbone really *is* a Guardian Angel. If it weren't for him, I'd have zoomed right off the stage and broken who knows what."

"Good boy, Wishbone!" Dropping to one knee, Joe ran his hand down Wishbone's back, then patted his side.

"You're lucky, Robin," Crystal said, standing at her seat below. "You could've really hurt yourself, like I did. Maybe your routine is too dangerous."

Amanda released a *tsk-tsk* of disapproval and shot Crystal a frown. "The dance routine is *safe!*" she insisted. "And so is Robin's skating routine. Maybe Joe or somebody should check out her skates!"

Sam exchanged glances with Joe.

"No problem," Joe said. As Robin pulled off her skates, Joe reached out and took them. "Maybe a little piece of something got wedged between a wheel and the body of the skate."

"Thanks, Joe," Robin said. As Joe headed offstage, Sam watched Ryan offer Robin a hand up.

Sam knew she had to talk to Crystal about what she had told Ryan and McKenzie yesterday at Pepper Pete's. From the corner of her eye, Sam saw McKenzie stomp offstage.

Ryan followed her. "Hey! Where are you going?"

McKenzie just kept walking, as if she didn't hear him.

I guess things haven't changed much since yesterday, Sam thought, as she headed down the stage steps. Smiling, she took a seat next to Crystal. "Hi."

"Hi, Sam." Crystal tucked a piece of loose hair behind her ear and smiled back.

Sam tried to think of a perfect way to start the conversation. She couldn't. Lowering her voice so no one else would hear, Sam dove right in. "I heard you were worried someone in the cast might get hurt."

Crystal tilted her head, a confused look on her face. "Who said that?"

What? Now Sam was confused. "Didn't you tell Ryan and McKenzie at Pepper Pete's that your fall wasn't an accident? That you thought someone *put* the scarf on the floor to make you slip?"

Crystal wrinkled her nose. "We were talking about David's sign. They must've misunderstood."

Where do I go from here? Sam wondered, eyeing Ryan and McKenzie. She glanced at Crystal. *Who's lying?*

Joe walked to the edge of the stage with one of Robin's skates in his hand. Looking at Sam, he flipped the skate upside down. "It was definitely sabotage," he said, spinning the wheels.

"Sabotage! That's terrible, Joe!" Wishbone had been enjoying the *'atta boy* scratches David was giving

92

him for saving Robin. But as the others slowly moved toward Joe, so did Wishbone and David.

Sam left her seat next to Crystal. "Joe, are you sure?" she asked, running up the stage steps.

Joe slowly spun the wheels on the skate one at a time. When he began to spin the third one in the line, it wobbled—*whump . . . whump . . . whump.*

"It's loose!" Sam watched Joe spin the wheel again, but faster. "But the axle bolts holding these wheels don't just *work* themselves loose. They have to be loosened with a special tool—an Allen key." She glanced at Robin. "Is yours here?"

Robin shook her head. "It's at home."

Sam exchanged looks with Joe. "But anybody who owns in-line skates owns an Allen key."

Joe nodded and handed Robin the skate.

"Bingo! That must be what I heard drop last night!" Wishbone watched the kids shoot suspicious looks at one another. "At least you can't blame this accident on me. I don't have any thumbs." He scratched his neck, then stood up. The kids were still looking at one another. "You know, there seems to be a lot of bad vibes around here. I think I'll wait this one out with my squeaky book."

Wishbone went back to the wings, where he'd left his toy. The floor was empty. He gasped.

"Squeaky?" Wishbone quickly sniffed back and forth across the area. Suddenly he recognized a scent. His head popped up. "Guys! Over here! *Both* stage invaders have struck again! And this time the ginger-snap thief stole my squeaky book!"

Not one of the kids looked Wishbone's way.

"Helllooo! Will *somebody* listen to the dog?"

Wishbone put all his senses on Red Alert.

"That cowardly dog! Nobody, *but nobody,* takes my squeaky book and gets away with it!" he said. "Now it's personal!"

Chapter Ten

More than a little worried, Sam looked at Justin to try to gauge his reaction to the sabotage. The way his head was tilted made his curls fall forward. With his rosy cheeks, he reminded Sam of an innocent angel. But his face told her nothing of how he felt.

Sam caught sight of Wishbone from the corner of her eye. He was quickly sniffing this way and that, as if he were hot on some kind of trail.

"Everybody go home," Justin said flatly. "Rehearsal's over."

What! Sam couldn't believe her ears.

Amanda clicked her tongue and sighed. No one else moved.

Justin glanced at his watch, then shook his wrist and looked again. Rubbing a hand across the back of his neck, he left through the curtained doorway.

Sam stared after him. *We're already way behind schedule. Now he's sending everyone home early.* "Wait!" Sam called, realizing some of the kids were starting to leave the stage. "Remember, tomorrow night is dress rehearsal. Everyone needs to be here by seven o'clock sharp, so you can get into full makeup and costume."

McKenzie looked as if she was getting impatient with Sam. *Now what is upsetting her?* thought Sam.

"We'll start right at seven-thirty," Sam continued, "and run through the play from start to finish—just as if it were opening night." Sam smiled. "'Bye."

Everyone started leaving.

Wishbone's head popped up as Joe and David started to walk out the auditorium doors. "I'll catch up with you at home, Joe. If the Allen key is anywhere around here, I want to find it."

With Joe and David gone, that left Sam, Justin, and Wishbone as the last ones in the auditorium. As Wishbone cocked his head and looked at Sam, she searched through the storage seat by the control panel. Then, with her eyes sweeping over the floor, she slowly walked across the stage.

"You're looking for something, too, huh, Sam?" Putting his nose to the floor, Wishbone sniffed. "You should really try using your nose more. . . . Hey!" He caught a whiff of canine scent. He followed it. But it disappeared, buried under a smudge of shoe prints. Picking up the scent a little farther on, Wishbone followed it as it faded in and out. "This trail is getting me nowhere fast."

Wishbone saw something out of the corner of his eye. It was on the floor, pressed up against the side of the storage seat that Sam had searched. He hurried over to examine it.

"Sam!" Wishbone barked. "This is it!" He barked again. "Helllooo! I could use a hand here. This is it! This is what I heard drop last night after the lights went out. Sam! Sam! Sam!" He barked louder.

Wishbone continued to bark as Sam walked his way.

She squinted and looked at the floor as she came near Wishbone. "The—"

"Be quiet!" Justin yelled through the curtained doorway. He then went through the doorway and stood in front of Sam. His face was red. He squeezed something so tightly in his hand that his fingers turned white. "How can I concentrate with all this noise? This play could've been perfect, but everybody ruined it!"

As Justin stepped toward Sam, Wishbone leaped between them. "Back off, buddy!"

Sam stared wide-eyed at Justin. "Wishbone found—"

Justin cut her off with a wave of his hand. As he spun around, he glanced into his hand at his watch. He threw the watch into the wastebasket by the curtained doorway. Then he pulled the curtain aside, stomped through the hallway, and out the backstage door.

Wishbone ran to the door. "And stay out!" he barked. Satisfied, he trotted back to Sam.

"Wow! Justin is really stressed," said Sam. She sighed and then glanced at her hand. In her open palm she held the Allen key.

Sam couldn't believe her luck. "Thanks, Wishbone! Too bad we don't know who it belongs to."

As Sam slipped the key into her pocket, she looked in the wastebasket. She picked up Justin's watch. The watch was running, but it was five minutes slow, and the crystal face was cracked.

"I guess it's not perfect, so he doesn't want it." Sam let it slip from her fingers, back into the trash. "Come on, Wishbone," she said. "I need to get my stuff from the dressing room. Then I want to talk to Joe and David."

As Sam walked toward David's house, she went over and over Justin's blow-up in her mind. *Why did he overreact like that?* It occurred to Sam that he had behaved in a way very similar to one of the suspects Miss Marple learned of in *Sleeping Murder.* Dr. Kennedy—Helen's brother—had told Miss Marple about an old boyfriend of Helen's. The man never got over his love for her, Dr. Kennedy said. This man was always very calm—except once, when he surprised everyone by exploding in a fit of temper over apparently nothing.

Sam's hand went to the Allen key in her jeans pocket. *Is Justin so afraid of the play being a flop that he's losing his cool? Is he the one sabotaging the play, stalling for time to improve the production?*

Considering everything that had already happened, it seemed that it would be impossible to open *Grease* on Friday night.

Chapter Eleven

"Hurry, Sam!" Wishbone called as he raced toward the Barnes's white picket fence. "Maybe we'll get there just in time for dinner." He waited for Sam on the front porch. "You go first . . . in case Emily answers the door." Wishbone wagged his tail as Sam rang the bell. "David's little sister finds me irresistible. But I don't think she's ever heard the saying 'If you love something, let it go.' She's more of the power-hugger type."

"Hmm . . ." After a short wait, Sam decided to knock on the door. "I'm sure the boys told me they were going right over to David's house."

"We could always wait for them in Wanda's yard." Wishbone pricked up his ears. "Wait! I hear something, Sam."

Suddenly the door opened. "Sam!" David said, sounding surprised. Under one arm was a small box marked CHRISTMAS LIGHTS.

Carrying a string of lights, Joe walked up behind

David. "Hi, Sam. I thought you were staying at the auditorium for a while longer."

"Hi, Joe. Hi, David." Wishbone nosed through the doorway, wagging his tail as he went. "Emily? You home?" he called.

"Hi, guys. Did you find replacement lights for David's sign?" asked Sam.

"We sure did." Joe held up the string of lights in his hands.

Sam stepped inside. "Good. I did stay after our short rehearsal. Wishbone and I both did—for a little while, anyway. You aren't going to believe what happened."

"What?" Joe asked curiously.

"I vote that we have this conversation in the kitchen," Wishbone said.

David set down the box he was carrying on the stairway. He motioned to them with his hand. "Let's go in the kitchen and have something to drink."

"Thank you, David!" Wishbone trotted alongside the kids. "Don't mind if I do."

"So tell us what happened," Joe said, as he and Sam sat in the chairs around the table.

Wishbone jumped up onto a chair, too. He looked over at David, who was pouring lemonade into glasses. "There's a bowl in the middle of the table, but the *dog* can't reach it, David! Water, please."

Sam set down her schoolbooks. Then she stretched out and pulled something out of her jeans pocket. She held it up. "Wishbone found the Allen key!"

"Good going, Wishbone!" Joe gave Wishbone a big smile.

Wishbone wagged his tail. "Thanks, Joe."

"Is there any way to tell whose it is?" David asked, bringing three full glasses to the table.

"No." Sam handed the key to Joe to look at. "But I suspect this key belongs to the saboteur. And if it does, it makes our sabotage theory more believable. And that's not all." Sam quickly removed her jacket. "Something weird happened with Justin. . . ."

David and Joe leaned in close to Sam. "And?" Joe asked.

"And David forgot to get me a drink," Wishbone said. "Excuse me." Wishbone jumped down to the floor. "Since no one's listening to the cute little dog, I think I'll snoop around down here for something tasty."

As Wishbone sniffed his way across the floor, he

listened to Sam tell Joe and David about Justin's outburst. Then she told the boys that she had found his watch in the garbage. Wishbone licked up a crumb so small that it was tasteless.

"You mean you think Justin might be the one behind the acts of sabotage?" Joe asked.

"Nothing, nothing, nothing." Wishbone continued to search. When he got to a corner of the room, he stopped and turned around. With his nose still hard at work, he started back across the floor. "Could someone point me in the direction of the flavorful crumbs?"

"He *could* be," Sam said. "He was disappointed that David and I did not agree with his production ideas for the sign. And putting Wishbone in a scene as the Guardian Angel was *his* idea. Those were his two biggest contributions, and both have been targeted by the saboteur. Maybe Justin tried to destroy them because they weren't working out the way he wanted them to—they were not up to his big expectations."

Sam thought of the events in *Sleeping Murder* again.

"You know, Miss Marple realized what she was up against when a newly installed tennis net was cut to shreds out of spite. Maybe Justin's being spiteful." She tilted her head. "And he's always been *on the spot.*"

Joe's brows wrinkled together as he looked at Sam. "What do you mean—'on the spot'?"

Sam started to explain. "In *Sleeping Murder,* Miss Marple digs into the disappearance of Helen. She's been missing for more than twenty years. But Helen's brother has letters from her that are dated after her disappearance. He even gets them checked out by a handwriting specialist. But Miss Marple still thinks there's something suspicious going on. So she makes a list of people who had a motive to kill Helen—a *reason* to commit murder—and she figures out which of them had the best opportunity to do it."

Joe nodded quickly. "In other words, she wanted to find out who was *on the spot.*"

"Correct," Sam said. "So, backing up a minute, who would want to interfere with the play?" She glanced from Joe to David. "If we can figure out who was on the spot for each incident, and then figure out who had the most to gain by the sabotage, I think we'll have the missing piece we need to see the whole picture."

"Doesn't Amanda have the biggest motive?" David asked. "She didn't get the lead role she wanted. And she was onstage when I brought the sign in. She was also there when Crystal slipped—"

"And she knew the exact line of Crystal's exit path from the stage," Joe added. "So she'd know where to place the scarf on the floor. Plus, we know she owns in-line skates. She'd definitely have an Allen key, and she could easily have loosened Robin's wheel."

Sam put a hand on her glass. "But the only incident she benefited from was Crystal's fall. Amanda is really proud of all her work." Sam brushed a piece of lint from her pants leg. "Besides, now that Amanda's performing Crystal's role, the sooner the play goes on, the better for her."

Joe shrugged his shoulders. David raised his eyebrows, but didn't answer.

"The one causing the trouble could even be Ryan," Sam said. "He was always *on the spot,* and he might want the play delayed. He still doesn't know all his lines."

"What about McKenzie?" Joe asked. "I bet she'd love to have the play be over with. Have you seen the look she gives to girls Ryan is nice to?"

"Yeah," David agreed. "She seems really jealous."

Sam nodded. "At first I thought McKenzie was giving Ryan those looks because she was upset that he was forgetting his lines. Then I realized she was jealous because all the girls think he's a nice guy."

Sam took a pretzel from the bowl in the center of the table.

"Ryan is sort of like another of Miss Marple's suspects in *Sleeping Murder*," Sam continued. "Girls just like him. Miss Marple wonders whether this guy's jealous wife had something to do with Helen's disappearance. He had always shown Helen a lot of attention."

"So which one's the murderer?" Joe asked eagerly.

Sam smiled. "I don't know yet. I'm not quite finished with the book." She tilted her head. "There is one more thing about Ryan and McKenzie. They told me Crystal didn't want me to know, but she's been worried about someone else in the cast getting hurt."

"I have a feeling there's more to that story," Joe said.

Glancing at her watch, Sam finished her lemonade. "Well, when I asked Crystal about it, she said she had no idea what I was talking about. She thinks Ryan and McKenzie got confused for some reason."

Joe looked at David, then Sam. "Do you think the two of them could be in on the sabotage together?"

Sam shrugged. "I don't know. But somebody's lying. Either Crystal, or Ryan and McKenzie." She got up from the table and set her empty glass in the sink. "Thanks, David. I think I'll stop by Pepper Pete's and see if my dad needs any help this evening."

Sam often worked weeknights at Pepper Pete's, doing her homework in between waiting on customers. When the restaurant closed that evening, she rode home with her dad.

"I'll be working late tonight in my office, Sam. I have to get the payroll done."

Sam smiled. "Okay, Dad." She went into the kitchen and set her books on the counter. Then she took a big red apple from the refrigerator. "I'll be reading *Sleeping Murder*," she called out to her dad as he headed for his office.

Grabbing the paperback from her stack of books, Sam hurried to the living room. She could hardly wait to begin reading. She was so close to the end—so close to finding out what happened to Helen. *If only I was that close to finding out what's happening at rehearsals!*

An hour later, Sam read the last line of the book. *Wow! So it turns out that Miss Marple has been right all along in her suspicions. Helen's letters have been faked, and Helen has really been murdered. And the crime was committed by the same man who had cut her tennis net to ribbons out of spite. It was Helen's brother, Dr. Kennedy, the man who was always making everyone else seem suspicious!*

Sam closed the book and placed it on the coffee table. All of a sudden, Sam felt her throat tighten. Now, thanks to Miss Marple, Sam thought she might finally know the identity of the saboteur. *And if I'm right, Amanda is in big trouble.*

Chapter Twelve

Thinking about who was responsible for the strange events that had occurred at rehearsals, Sam tossed and turned all night. When her alarm went off Thursday morning, she quickly ate breakfast, then called Joe. "Hi. It's Sam," she said. "Did I wake you?"

"No," Joe said. "Is something wrong?"

Sam didn't answer him directly. "Can you and David meet me at my locker first thing this morning? I have something important I want to talk to you guys about."

"Sure," Joe said.

"Great. How about ten minutes before the first-period bell?"

"I'll call David and tell him," Joe said.

"Thanks, Joe. 'Bye." Sam hung up the phone, then finished getting ready for school. *How am I ever going to prove my suspicions?* Sam wondered, as she pulled her hair back into a ponytail. Finally, she put on her jacket. After scooping up her books, she peeked into her dad's office. "'Bye, Dad. See you later."

Walter Kepler looked up from his desk and smiled. "Have a nice day, Sam. See you after school."

Sam left the house and hurried to school.

Inside, she passed a small group of boys talking in the hall. One of them was Ryan. "Hi," she said, smiling.

"Sam!" Ryan broke away from the group and came over to her. He had a desperate look on his face. "I have a big, big favor to ask you. McKenzie isn't here today, and I always practice my lines with her. Will you help me at lunch?"

"Sure," Sam said. "I'll see you then." Sam saw a look of relief pass over Ryan's face. With dress rehearsal that night, he still wasn't sure of his lines. No wonder he looked so desperate—but was the pressure on him enough to cause him to sabotage the play and give himself more time?

Sam continued on through the hall and then put her stuff into her locker. Just as she was pulling out the books she needed for her first class, Joe and David came up beside her.

"Hey, what's all this about something important you need to tell us?" David asked, tucking a shoe box under his arm.

As kids dug through their lockers on both sides of her, Sam looked for a more private place to talk. "Over here." She walked to a corner near the stairway, then spoke in a low voice. "I think I may know who's behind all the trouble at rehearsals."

"Justin?" David guessed.

Sam nodded. "Could be. He's such a perfectionist. If the play isn't perfect, he might want it canceled. But he wasn't even close to being *on the spot* when Crystal slipped on the scarf. He was sitting out in the auditorium with me."

"Ryan?" Joe suggested.

"He *has* been acting very guilty since Crystal's fall," Sam said. "And he's very nervous about not knowing his lines. But the rest just doesn't fit."

"McKenzie?" Joe and David whispered at the same time.

"She's been very unhappy watching Ryan rehearse with all those other girls," Sam admitted. "It makes me think of something Miss Marple says in *Sleeping Murder*. Ryan doesn't mean to make McKenzie jealous. She's the one he likes the most. She can't help being jealous, so they're both miserable. But is she jealous enough to ruin the play?"

David and Joe exchanged glances. "That takes care of everyone, doesn't it?" Joe asked.

"There *is* one more suspect." Sam shifted the books in her arms. "I finished reading *Sleeping Murder* last night. Helen really *was* murdered, just as Miss Marple thought. Miss Marple finally put all the pieces together. The only one who said Helen hadn't been murdered was her brother, Dr. Kennedy—because he was the one who murdered her."

Joe's eyebrows shot up in surprise. "But why did he kill her?"

"Wait!" David said. "Remember the tennis net that was cut to pieces? Did Dr. Kennedy cut that up, too?"

"Right," Sam said. "Miss Marple called it a nasty bit of spite. And that wasn't all he did that was mean. He faked letters supposedly written by Helen, saying she had run away. He made everyone look guilty, especially Helen, who was dead and couldn't defend herself."

"But who's behind all the spiteful pranks at rehearsals?" Joe asked. "The pink scarf, David's sign, Robin's skate. Each incident seems to be getting more dangerous."

Before Sam could answer, the first-period bell rang. Kids swarmed toward their classrooms.

"We haven't even been to our lockers yet," David said. "Come on, Joe."

"But Sam hasn't told us yet who she thinks the saboteur is," Joe said. "Meet us at lunch," he called, walking backward toward his locker.

"I can't," Sam said, remembering she'd promised to help Ryan with his lines. "How about meeting in the auditorium after school?"

"Okay," David called, as Sam went one way, and he and Joe continued to move the other way.

"Well, it's been nice talking to you," Wishbone said to the man sitting next to him on the park bench. "But I have to get to rehearsal now." He wagged his tail and jumped down to the sidewalk. "Thanks for sharing your banana bread with me." Wishbone trotted a few steps away, and then he stopped. "I hope you can see the play."

Wishbone trotted toward Sequoyah Middle School. As he made his way there, he felt frustrated by his lack of progress in his criminal investigation.

"I hope Sam has had better luck finding out who's trying to destroy the play than I have had in finding the ginger-snap thief."

As he approached the big double front doors to the school, the groups of students made room for him to pass through. "Hey, look at that," he said, heading inside. "I guess they know a star when they see one." Wishbone sat by a wall, waiting for the hubbub of dismissal to die down. Then he spotted his best buddy. "Hey, Joe—over here!"

When Joe didn't answer, Wishbone followed him. He weaved his way down the hall among the students.

"Excuse me, excuse me . . . Oops! Sorry about that. Hey! Walk on your own two feet, not my four."

Finally the crowd thinned out. Wishbone caught up with Joe at the same time David did.

"Wishbone, what are you doing here?" Joe asked, when he spotted the dog.

"Well!" Wishbone sat down. "Let me just say it's nice to see you, too, Joe."

"There's no practice after school today—we have dress rehearsal at seven o'clock tonight."

Wishbone wagged his tail. "I don't wear a watch, Joe. I tell time by daily routine—meal times, nap times, snack times, and play times. So if you could be a little more specific—"

David started walking again. "Nobody will be bothered by him. He can go with us."

"I'd love to. Go where?" Wishbone asked. "Hey, wait for me!" He took off after Joe when Joe started to walk down the hall. When Joe stopped at the familiar doors of the auditorium and began to let himself inside, Wishbone cocked his head. "I thought you said there was no rehearsal after school."

Sam stood on the stage and looked around. The bleachers were set up for the big dance scene. All the Grease kids would be celebrating the last day of school. Sam couldn't help but get excited. Tomorrow was opening night for the play!

Suddenly the auditorium doors flew open. In came Joe, David, and Wishbone. "Hi! Come on in!" Sam waited for them to climb the steps to the stage.

"Okay," Joe said. "Besides Ryan, McKenzie, and Justin, who else could be sabotaging the play?"

As Wishbone wandered across the stage, Sam looked from Joe to David. "Crystal."

"Crystal?" David said. "But she was the first person to get hurt. She couldn't have caused her own accident, could she?"

"David's right," Joe said. "And she was always looking out for everyone else, so they wouldn't get hurt, too."

Sam frowned. "I'm not sure how the scarf got out of the wardrobe closet. But there's something I've noticed about Crystal. First she said I told her the wrong time for that rehearsal. I don't know, maybe I did. But maybe I didn't. Then she said Amanda's dance on the bleachers wasn't safe."

Sam walked back to the bleachers and sat down at one end of the lowest bench. The boys followed her. David climbed to the bench above, while Joe sat next to Sam.

"Then," Sam said, reaching down to scratch Wishbone when he came over and put a paw on her leg, "there's that incident with Ryan and McKenzie. They said Crystal told them she was worried about someone else in the cast getting hurt. But when I asked her about it, she claimed that she didn't know anything at all about it."

The bleacher seat squeaked as David made himself comfortable.

"It took me a while to realize it," Sam said, "but something didn't seem right. I finally realized there was sort of a pattern with Crystal."

"What kind of pattern?" Joe asked.

Resting her hands on her knees, Sam watched Wishbone trot over to the back of the bleachers. "She always sounded so nice—so nice you almost didn't notice that what she was really doing was . . . warning us of what was to come next."

"Yeah." David leaned forward, making his bleacher bench squeak again. "Like when my sign threw sparks, it was Crystal who was afraid it would happen opening night and someone would get hurt."

"Right," Sam said. "And when Robin fell, Crystal said the skates were dangerous and that Robin could get hurt, *just the way she did.*" Sam noticed that Wishbone was snooping underneath the bleachers at the other end from where she sat.

Joe waved a finger in the air. "And Ryan and McKenzie said Crystal warned them about sabotage occurring on opening night—and then Crystal said they were mistaken. It seemed like Ryan and McKenzie were lying."

115

Sam nodded, looking from Joe to David. "Crystal was always on the spot. We just didn't consider her as a suspect because of her injured ankle."

"All of this is still not definite proof," David said. "But I think you've found the missing piece, Sam."

Suddenly, Sam bolted straight up. "There's something else!" she said excitedly. "Remember Tuesday night, when we came back to the school in the storm? There were no wet footprints inside the door, but there was somebody else there in the auditorium with us. Wishbone proved it when he found the Allen key. The intruder would've had to use the front doors to get in—the backstage door doesn't have a handle on the outside. Crystal was the only one who left Pepper Pete's *before* it started raining!"

As the boys stood up, Wishbone let out a bark.

"Wishbone agrees with you." Joe smiled.

"The thing is," said Sam, "if I'm right, Amanda will be the next victim. Crystal wants to make doubly sure Amanda doesn't play Sandy on opening night. I'm just not sure how she's going to do it."

Wishbone barked again, growling at the back of the bleachers.

"What's the matter, Wishbone?" David asked. Taking a quick step to the end of the bleachers, David jumped off. The opposite end of the bench wobbled up and down like a stiff diving board.

Wishbone jumped up and barked again.

Joe hurried to Wishbone's end of the bleachers. He looked in the direction of where the dog was barking. Then Joe checked out the bench. "Look at this. All the nails in the wooden planks at this end of the bench are missing. I think Wishbone's figured out what was going to happen to Amanda. She and Ryan are supposed to dance on these bleachers!"

Sam pointed a finger in the air. "I think I know how to turn the situation around and catch Crystal in her own trap."

Chapter Thirteen

When Wishbone, Joe, and David pushed through the auditorium doors for dress rehearsal, Crystal and Justin were already there, on the stage.

"Cool!" Wishbone wagged his tail and trotted up the stage steps. The stage was set up for scene one—part of the schoolyard and parking lot. The bleachers had been pulled forward. Behind them were scenery props of neat old cars. Red, black, and yellow cars. Even a pink one.

As soon as Joe made his way into the wings and turned on the rest of the stage lights, Wishbone stood at the edge of the stage.

Crystal slowly walked down the steps and took a seat in the front of the auditorium. Ryan and McKenzie, then Robin, entered through the auditorium doors. Wishbone wagged his tail to show them they'd been noticed. Then Amanda came in.

Wishbone scratched his neck with his hind paw. "I don't know why they have to play a recording along with me. I have a terrific voice!" Wishbone stood and shook, trying to cool himself off. "Wow!" He glanced toward the ceiling. "Having all these bright stage lights on makes it hot up here—sort of like sitting in a car on a warm, sunny day." He looked around. "And there's no window here for me to stick my head out of to get a breath of fresh air."

Wishbone looked out over the seats in the auditorium as the doors in back opened again. Sam hurried in, her ponytail swinging back and forth.

"Sam!" Wagging his tail, Wishbone greeted her when she got to the top of the steps.

Sam gave him an unusually quick head scratch. "Sorry, Wishbone, I'm in a hurry."

He could tell. Sam was on a mission. And it probably had something to do with the rehearsal prankster. "I think I'll just tag along, Sam."

"Joe, have you seen Justin?" Sam asked hurriedly.

"He went through there." Joe pointed to the curtained doorway. "He must be in the dressing room or the storage room." He raised his eyebrows. "Good luck."

"Thanks," Sam said. Glancing over her shoulder, Sam quickly disappeared through the curtained doorway.

Wishbone followed her. "Hey!" He started to growl at the stranger in the hallway. Then he realized it was Ryan, with Crystal. Ryan's hair was slicked straight back. "Wow! Whatever you have in your hair makes it glisten like a wet street on a rainy night." The dog eyed Ryan's tight white T-shirt. Something was rolled up in one of the sleeves. "And look at those jeans you're wearing! They fit tighter than an outgrown collar. I couldn't tug on one of those pant legs without getting your skin in my teeth!"

Crystal had her hair pulled into a high ponytail. It was tied with a pink scarf. Other than that, she had on her regular school clothes.

Ryan and Crystal disappeared through the curtained doorway to the stage.

Peeking into the dressing room, Wishbone saw Sam and Justin. He pricked up his ears and listened while Sam explained to Justin why she thought Crystal was the person responsible for the pranks. Then Sam told Justin why she needed to make a slight change in the rehearsal.

Justin nodded his head. But as Sam walked back toward the stage, Wishbone sensed she was feeling uncomfortable.

"Something tells me that taking your hand and making a few long, slow strokes from my head to my tail would make you feel better," Wishbone said. "Come on, just try it." He wagged his tail as he walked at Sam's side. "Who knows? Maybe I'll feel better, too."

But Sam walked over and stood in the center of the stage. She stopped and positioned herself facing away from the empty auditorium. "This is it, guys," she called to the other kids. "Let's get started."

Wishbone watched the cast members gather around Sam. Rachel and Robin were dressed all in pink—including their shoes. "Now I understand why you're called the Pink Ladies in the play!"

Suddenly, Justin stood beside Sam. When the talking died down, Sam spoke to the cast. "I know we said we were going to run through the play from start to finish tonight," she said. "And we're still sticking to that plan. But there is one slight change."

"What's that?" Ryan stuck his thumbs in his belt loops and shifted his weight to one leg.

"Hey, Ryan! You look just like one of the guys I saw in the movie version of *Grease!*" Wishbone wagged his tail.

Justin glanced at Sam for a moment. Then he spoke to the kids. "Before we start the run-through," he said, "we're going to do the dance finale with Crystal, instead of Amanda, playing Sandy."

Wishbone heard Amanda suck in her breath. *"What?"*

Justin held up a hand to cut her off. "That way," he continued, "if Crystal's ankle is okay, she can be Sandy for the entire dress rehearsal. You know, that will be a good way for her to sort of refresh her memory for her part."

Without another word, Justin turned and walked down the stage steps to take his place in the first row of the auditorium seats.

"Ooh," Wishbone said, watching Amanda. "You look angry . . . *and* surprised—just like a cornered cat."

"But, Sam," Crystal said, "I'm not even in costume. You said Amanda was going to be doing the role of Sandy in the dress rehearsal, remember?"

"Right!" Amanda frowned and crossed her arms in front of her.

Sam smiled as she stood at the center of the stage. "I know, Crystal, but Justin really wants to try this first. It's just to see if you can handle such a big role on opening night." Then, with a glance to Justin in the front row, Sam waved her arm. "Okay, everybody clear the stage for Crystal and Ryan."

In a thundering of footsteps, the kids immediately hurried off the stage. Wishbone's ears picked up Amanda's steps over the rest. Her steps were more of a stomp. Then he noticed Crystal still lingering onstage near Sam.

"What's the matter?" Sam asked Crystal. She asked the question so quietly that it was almost a whisper.

Wishbone tilted his head to hear Sam's words better. He knew the other kids couldn't hear her at all.

Crystal glanced at the floor. "Nothing. I'll get changed."

"Nothing?" Wishbone cocked his head as he watched her walk away. "That's not what I'm sensing." A moth flew past his muzzle. Wishbone snapped, but purposely missed. "You're in my space, buddy." He watched the moth fly upward to the lights and flutter back and forth for a while. Then he watched it spiral downward, flutter, and spiral downward some more. "Lucky for you I'm only into chasing cats."

A few minutes later, Crystal was back onstage wearing pink jeans, a pink sweater, and pink shoes.

"Places, everyone!" Sam called as she settled down in the front row of seats.

Ryan stood on one side of the stage, with one foot up on the bleachers. His back was to the auditorium. Crystal waited in the wings on the other side of the stage. Joe turned off the auditorium lights, then the stage lights.

A second later the stage lights came back on. Crystal-as-Sandy strutted across the stage toward Ryan-as-

Danny. Sandy now looked completely different from the way she had on the first day of school. This was the real Sandy. She'd slipped off her short leash and now she was free to be herself and have fun. She was out-cooling the top dog of cool—and Danny loved it!

"Wow!" Wishbone said as he watched her. "You can waggle just like Wiggles, this cocker spaniel I know."

Crystal spun Ryan around to face her.

"Sandy?" Ryan raised his eyebrows in surprise.

When she nodded, he broke into a huge grin. "Cool!"

"Yeah, cool!" said Wishbone. "And speaking of cool, where's that breeze coming from?" Wishbone raised his head in surprise as another moth flew by him on the winter breeze. *Moth? Breeze? That's it! That's how the ginger-snap-stealing, squeaky-book-kidnapping dog got in here!* He glanced in Joe's direction. *The backstage door!*

As the music started and Ryan took one of Crystal's hands in his, Wishbone belly-crawled back closer to Joe and David. He could still see most of the stage. And with just a quick glance, he could see through the curtained doorway to the backstage door. *Okay, you canine crook, I'm ready for you now!*

Ryan twirled Crystal under his arm. Then he jumped up on the bleachers to dance. But instead of Crystal jumping up, too, she let go of Ryan's hand.

Wishbone cocked his head. "Uh . . . Crystal . . . I think you forgot to pick up your feet."

David stopped the music. Crystal looked out at Sam and Justin and smiled. "Just for tonight I'm going

123

to do my dance routine on the floor, instead of up on the bleachers."

"Actually," Sam said, "we need to see you in action on the bleachers."

Crystal glanced at the bleachers. "I can't."

"Don't worry, Crystal, you'll do just great," Ryan reassured her. "Just like always."

Crystal shook her head firmly. "I can't."

"Sure you can!" Robin said.

Crystal looked at the floor in front of her feet. "I don't want to."

"Come on. I won't let you fall." Ryan stepped down to the floor and held out his hand, but Crystal didn't take it. "I'll tell you what. If you start to fall, I'll throw myself on the floor and be your cushion."

"I can't!" Crystal snapped, glaring at him.

Sam got up from her seat and took a step closer to the stage. She spoke gently. "Why don't you tell him why not, Crystal."

Crystal's face became red as she turned toward Sam.

Sam didn't let Crystal's angry stare bother her.

"What's Sam talking about?" Ryan asked Crystal. A murmur spread all across the stage and in the wings as all eyes turned to Crystal.

Sam hurried up the steps to the stage. The kids in the wings came out onstage, surprised by the sudden turn of events.

"The bleachers aren't safe to dance on," Crystal said softly.

"Why not?" asked Ryan, as he shook his head in confusion. "They were fine before."

"I took some nails out of them," Crystal said, her glance darting from one face to another.

"What!" exclaimed Ryan.

"She said she rigged the bleachers so we would fall," Amanda said angrily. "And I will bet she tampered with Robin's skate and David's sign the same way!"

"Is that true, Crystal?" Sam asked.

Crystal didn't say anything.

Joe pointed to the "Greased Lightning" sign over his head. "Did you cut the wiring on David's sign?"

"I didn't mean to make it spark and burn the way it did," Crystal blurted out. "I heard someone coming before I could cut all the way through all the wires. I wanted it just not to work until opening night."

"I had to rewire the whole thing," David said, annoyed. "Joe and I just got it hung up again."

Robin shook her head in amazement. "I can't believe you loosened the wheel on my skate. If it wasn't for Wishbone, I would've been hurt."

"I just thought the skate wouldn't work right," Crystal said. "I never thought you'd be in any real danger, Robin."

"So you did that the night of the storm, when we moved the props from the art room to the stage?" Sam asked.

Crystal sighed. "I sneaked out the backstage door when I heard you and Joe and David come into the auditorium."

The kids waited silently for Crystal to continue.

"And you fixed the bleachers so I would get hurt," Amanda announced. "That's really dangerous, Crystal.

125

The bleachers would've collapsed right while I was dancing on them."

"Along with me," Ryan added.

"And the play would have been canceled for sure," Justin said, giving Crystal an angry stare.

"Canceled?" Crystal repeated, shocked. "I never even thought of that happening. I didn't really hurt my ankle that badly. I knew I'd be fine by opening night. I was just livening up rehearsals until then. It was all just a joke."

"Livening up rehearsals?" Sam said. The rest of the cast moaned in disbelief. "You think sabotaging the play was just a game?"

Crystal looked around the stage at the angry cast. "You have to admit it was a good joke," she said. "Rehearsals were getting pretty boring. I knew *my* lines."

Looking at Crystal, Sam said, "You're the star of the show. Wasn't that enough attention for you? Did you really need more?"

When Crystal didn't say anything, Sam knew she had guessed right.

Sam suddenly remembered how all this trouble had started. "I didn't really tell you the wrong time for rehearsal on Monday, did I?" she asked.

"I wanted to make a big entrance that day," said Crystal with a shrug. "I'm sorry if I scared anyone, but nobody got hurt. The play's going to be better than ever. You'll see. I'll be the best Sandy ever on opening night."

"Not in my production. I will be reporting this to the principal. You could have hurt someone really badly, Crystal," Justin said flatly. "Amanda, I know this is very late notice, but would you consider taking over the lead role of Sandy on opening night?"

Amanda enjoyed the moment for as long as she could. Then she smiled broadly. "I'd be glad to!"

"You're kidding, right?" Crystal asked Justin. "I'm the best actor you have in the cast. I've been to every rehearsal!"

"Crystal, I agree with Justin," Sam said. "You not only risked the success of the play, but you placed several people in danger. I think Amanda will make a great Sandy. She's proven that she puts the play first, before herself. You proved just the opposite."

Crystal's bottom lip started to quiver as she slowly pulled the pink scarf from her ponytail and handed it to Amanda. She seemed close to tears. "I never meant

for all of this trouble to happen. I didn't mean to hurt anyone, and I'm really sorry," she said.

All of a sudden, Wishbone stiffened and let out a low growl.

Raising her eyebrows, Robin eyed Wishbone. "What's wrong with the Guardian Angel?"

Sam exchanged glances with Joe.

"What's the matter, boy?" Joe asked, as Wishbone stared toward the curtained doorway.

"Wait a minute." Scowling, Justin held up a hand. "We still have one remaining mystery." He looked at Sam. "How did the scarf Crystal slipped on get on the floor in the first place?"

Wishbone let out another growl, then raced off.

"Joe! Sam!" Wishbone barked as he headed directly to the curtained doorway. "This way, everyone! I saw a brown flash, and my nose tells me the canine crook is just through here." He looked back at the kids. Sam, Joe, and the others were hot on his trail. "I'm going to get this brute if it takes me all night!" he barked.

As Wishbone turned back around to bolt through the doorway, he saw brown fluff exiting through the backstage door. A book held the door open just a crack. Wishbone stuck his nose in the crack and pushed.

"Ugh!" He tried to squeeze through, but couldn't. "Joe!" He barked toward the door handle. "Give me a hand."

Picking up the book, Joe swung the door open wide. "Thanks, buddy!" Wishbone rushed outside into the chilly, dark night. He could see his breath come out of his mouth in quick, white puffs. "Come out, come out, wherever you are! You squeaky-book-stealing crook!" He put his nose to the ground and sniffed the cold, damp grass. He picked up a fresh scent. "Super Dog is on the way!"

"What's he running after?" McKenzie asked.

Joe kept following him. "Beats me, but it must be pretty important."

Wishbone's nose led him from one bush to another. At the fourth bush, he stiffened. "Stand back!" Wishbone warned the kids. "My nose tells me the canine crook is hiding back under here. He might be dangerous—I'll go in alone."

"I think he's found something," Joe said, as Wishbone dropped to his belly and crawled under the bush.

"I most certainly have!" Wishbone said. "You should see all the stuff back here. Oh! Squeaky book!" Grabbing it in his mouth, Wishbone scooted out of the bush backward.

A furry brown puff about Wishbone's size came skipping out after him. It tried to lick his face.

"Hey! Don't get so personal. We haven't even met yet!" Wishbone said.

"Oh, a puppy! He's so cute!" Robin bent down to pick it up, but the puppy ran to Ryan.

"She," Ryan said, as the pup leaned her front paws on Ryan's pants leg. Scooping her up, Ryan cuddled the pup in his arms. She crawled up and licked his face and ear. "Everybody, meet Jinx. She's mine." Ryan held her up for all the kids to see. Then he looked into the dog's eyes. "I had a feeling you might be in on this."

129

When he set her on the ground, she ran straight to Wishbone. "I'm really sorry," he said. "She has a number of bad habits. For one, she likes to steal things."

"That's not exactly news," Wishbone said, keeping his squeaky book safely between his front paws.

Jinx let out a yip and wagged her tail at Wishbone. Wishbone looked at her. "My guess is half German shepherd, and half Irish setter."

Ryan nodded at the bush. "I bet she's got a stash of stuff back there."

David bent down. "I can't see anything." Reaching his hand in, he scooped out a pile of things.

"Hey!" Joe snatched up a piece of paper. "This is part of the wrapper from my missing energy bar." He petted Wishbone. "Sorry, boy. The evidence sure made you *look* guilty."

"I know. But things aren't always what they seem." He wagged his tail. "Apology accepted, Joe."

Jinx nudged Wishbone, then licked his nose. Her long tail whipped back and forth.

"Okay," Wishbone finally admitted to the adoring puppy. "I forgive you, too. Now, quit washing my face. And if we're going to be friends, there's one thing you should know—nobody touches squeaky but me! Oh, and one more thing." He wagged his tail. "How do you feel about pepperoni pizza?"

"Look how Jinx is sitting," Joe said. "It looks like she's trying to copy Wishbone."

"Well, I hope she picks up some of his good habits." Ryan sounded hopeful. "Jinx also likes to chew on just about anything."

Wishbone sat taller. "I'm a perfect role model!"

"Yeah." David held up a piece of shoelace from Jinx's stash. Then he pulled a small pink scarf out of the dirt. "It's hard to see in this light, but I think there's a bunch of holes in this—just like the holes in the scarf Crystal slipped on."

"So it was Jinx who left the scarf on the stage floor!" Sam said.

Chapter Fourteen

Friday evening passed faster than Wishbone would have liked. Standing in the wings next to Sam, the Jack Russell terrier watched the final scene of *Grease*. He wagged his tail.

"I love this part!" he said excitedly. "Everyone's together, dancing, having the best time just playing their parts!" He looked back at Joe, standing at the control panel.

"Hear that applause?" Wishbone asked as the curtain closed. "The audience loved us!" He flipped. "Hey, Sam, do you think there are any critics out there? I bet we get a four-bone review."

"Curtain call!" Sam announced in a hushed voice, as Joe started to open the curtain again. "Wishbone, you go first."

Wishbone cocked his head. "Go first and do what, Sam?"

"Go on!" Sam encouraged him. "Stand at the edge of the stage. Take a bow and enjoy the applause."

"Oh, right. I remember!" Wishbone trotted out to the front edge of center stage.

The stage lights were so bright that the dog could see only the first few rows of people. The rest of the auditorium looked black, but he sensed by the sounds that the room was packed. As he took his bow, the clapping got louder.

Wishbone lowered his voice to sound like the popular 1950s rock-and-roll singer Elvis Presley. "Thank you. Thank you very much." He spotted Joe's mom and their next-door neighbor in the second row. "Hi, Ellen! Hi, Wanda! Nice hat." Then he saw Walter Kepler and the Barnes family, too. "Hi, guys! Was I a great Guardian Angel, or what?" Then he spotted Crystal clapping, too.

After the play, instead of going to the cast party with the other kids, Crystal would be collecting the props and sweeping up the auditorium. After that, she still had a week's worth of detention after school. *She's really in the dog house,* Wishbone thought.

The clapping got louder and louder every time another actor came out onstage and took a bow.

"Wow!" Wishbone said when the stars, Ryan and Amanda, came out together, held hands, and bowed. "Listen to that applause! This could be hard on the ears." He wagged his tail. "But it sure does wonders for the ego."

Above him, the lights on David's "Greased Lightning" sign brightened and flashed—the way they were supposed to—to signal the end of the curtain call. This time whistles and roars went through the crowd.

Crystal got out of her seat and walked up to the

edge of the stage. With all the noise, even Wishbone could barely hear what she said to Amanda—it sounded like *good job*.

Wishbone was disappointed when the curtain began to close. "Oh, well. All good things must come to an end. Now, let's celebrate!" he said when the curtain was shut and the clapping had stopped. "Start the cast party!"

"Great job, everyone!" Sam said, as she and Justin joined the cast onstage.

"Ditto," Justin said to the kids. "I wasn't sure we could pull this thing off. But we did." He pointed a thumb at Sam. "Our stage manager, here, was the major reason for our success."

Suddenly Wishbone pricked up his ears. "Someone's knocking on the backstage door!" He barked and raced through the curtained doorway.

Justin and Sam followed him.

Unlocking the door, Justin pushed it open. "Hi."

"Delivery from Pepper Pete's," a girl's voice said from behind a stack of boxes.

Wishbone sucked in his breath and wagged his tail. "Look at all that pizza! Oh, I just love a celebration!" He walked back and forth impatiently while Sam and Justin took the boxes from the delivery girl. "Tip her, Justin," Wishbone said, "and let's party!"

Just as the door was about to close, a brown ball of fluff shot through the doorway.

"Jinx!" Sam and Justin sounded surprised.

Bounding up to Wishbone, Jinx wagged her tail and swiped her tongue across his muzzle. Then she licked his ear.

"Come on, cut it out," Wishbone said. "That tickles, and you're embarrassing me." He turned his head to avoid another lick. "I hope you don't mind, Sam, but I invited a guest."

Sam laughed. "I think she's Wishbone's guest."

"Helllooo! I just said that." Wishbone turned to Jinx. "The first thing you should know, Jinx, is that nobody ever listens to the dog." He started to move away from the door. "Come on, Jinx. Follow me. I'll show you the polite way to get food from humans. It's called begging."

Sam and Justin followed the dogs through the doorway leading to the stage.

"Pizza's here!" Justin called. "And there are soft drinks and juice in the red ice chest by the control panel."

Amanda, Robin, and some of the other cast members went in that direction. Meanwhile, Joe and David grabbed chairs. Then they followed Sam and Justin to the bleachers, where they set down the pizza boxes.

"Jinx!" Ryan sounded surprised to see his dog.

"It's okay," Wishbone assured him. "She's with me."

Ryan looked at McKenzie. Then they both gazed at the dogs and laughed.

"What?" Wishbone asked, wondering what was so funny. "Oh, never mind." He turned around. "Come on, Jinx. Sam, David, and Joe are in the corner, and they have at least one slice of pizza each."

The terrier trotted toward them, with the puppy at his side.

"Stop and sit," Wishbone told Jinx when they were close and facing all three of the kids. "These are my people, and right now they are deep in conversation! They like to share food. . . . Okay, *most* of the time they like to share. But it doesn't hurt to look cute."

Wishbone wagged his tail in order to get Jinx's full attention.

"Do it like this, Jinx. Just tilt your head to one side, keep your big brown eyes fixed on their eyes, and then lift your front paws off the ground." He showed her. "See? It's called begging. It's much more polite than stealing. Hmm . . ." He eyed his new friend. "I can see we're going to have to work on the front-paws-off-the-ground routine. Stick with me, kid!"

Sam looked down and saw Wishbone sitting up in his well-mannered begging position. "Look, guys," she said to Joe and David. "Wishbone and Jinx want some pizza, too." She tore off a piece of her sausage pizza for Wishbone. Then she gave Jinx a piece of the crust.

"You're still a puppy, Jinx. I don't think you should have the cheese and meat yet."

Joe looked at Sam. "You really did a great job—with *Grease* . . . *and* with our mystery."

"Thanks." Sam grinned as she looked from Joe to David. "I had a little help from my friends. Oh." Sam held up a finger. "And from Miss Marple, too."

"That's all you went by to figure out that the stage invader was Crystal—the Miss Marple book?" Joe asked.

Sam shook her head. "No, but I think that was what headed me in the right direction. Crystal always seemed so concerned about others, so I never gave her a second thought. But after reading *Sleeping Murder,* I realized that what Crystal was really doing was trying to make others look guilty. It was the same thing Dr. Kennedy did in the book."

Sam finished her pizza, then wiped her hands on a napkin.

Sam continued: "When things first started going wrong, I wished *I* had a Guardian Angel. Then I finally started to trust my own instincts. I could do it all along—I just had to believe it."

She glanced from Joe to David. She could tell they were ready to go back for more pizza.

"Now my instincts are telling me something else," Sam said, jumping up first. Sam smiled as she, Joe, and David headed toward the nearest pizza box.

About Vivian Sathre

This is Vivian Sathre's fourth WISHBONE book. Her previous books are *Wishbone's Dog Days of the West*, a Super Adventures of Wishbone book; *Dog Overboard!* and *Digging Up the Past*, both Adventures of Wishbone books. Vivian has been writing for thirteen years. Although she has written many books, including picture books and chapter books for young readers, this current story, *Stage Invader*, is the first mystery story she has written. She found it to be a great challenge. But just as students have teachers to guide them in the right direction, writers have editors who guide them in the creative process, too. Vivian is grateful for the help her editors gave her with *Stage Invader*. She says that without their help it would have been impossible for her to write this story.

Writing WISHBONE books is a lot of fun for Vivian. Maybe that's because she feels she has a few things in common with Wishbone. She, too, loves a good book *and* a good snack. Also, just like Wishbone, she always tries to look at life with a positive attitude. It makes life so much more fun! Vivian also has at least one thing in common with Sam, Joe, and David. When Vivian was in the ninth grade, she also attended a school named Sequoia—same name, different spelling!

While Vivian was growing up, her family almost always had a dog. There was Sparky, Lady, Auggie, and Flip. None was fluent in the English language the way

Wishbone is. But when it came to canine-speak—growling and barking—they had it down pat.

Vivian lives in the Seattle, Washington, area with her husband and teenaged sons. They have two cats. Vivian and her cats watch WISHBONE almost every day on PBS.

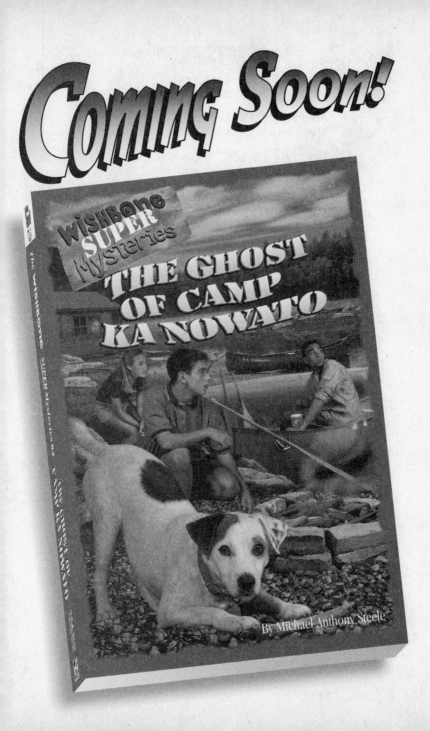

The Adventures of WISHBONE™

Read all the books in
The Adventures of Wishbone™ series!

Read all the books in the
WISHBONE™ Mysteries series!

WHAT HAS FOUR LEGS, A HEALTHY COAT, AND A GREAT DEAL ON MEMBERSHIP?

IT'S THE **WISHBONE**™ ZONE
THE OFFICIAL **WISHBONE** FAN CLUB!

When you enter the **WISHBONE ZONE,** you get:
- Color poster of **Wishbone**™
- A one-year subscription to *The WISHBONE ZONE News*– that's at least four issues of the hottest newsletter around!
- Autographed photo of **Wishbone** and his friends
- **WISHBONE** sunglasses, and more!

To join the fan club, pay $10 and charge your **WISHBONE ZONE** membership to VISA, MasterCard, or Discover. Call:

1-800-888-WISH

Or send us your name, address, phone number, birth date, and a check for $10 payable to Big Feats! (TX residents add $.83 sales tax). Write to:

WISHBONE ZONE
P.O. Box 9523
Allen, TX 75013-9523

Prices and offer are subject to change. Place your order now!